Dreamers

Life on Ooba

RYAN WARNER

DREAMERS

Contents

Zazri

"Run Skade, get out of here."

"No, I can't leave you."

"Son, you need to go, save our family and the dreamers, and if you're going to make it you need to leave now." As I heard my father say these words, I knew that he was right and that there wasn't any other way. I took a in a deep breath and a long look at my father with great sorrow in my eyes knowing that I would never see him again. He gave me a little smile. I could feel the love he had for me when I looked into his eyes. This expression gave me the assurance that it would all be okay and the courage to do as he asked.

I turned and I immediately ran for the back of the house, passing through the living room with our nice blue flower printed carpet that was as soft as an ocean breeze. Our family table that my dad had made was sitting on top of it with some freshly picked peaches in a nice wooden box. The wooden box had my dad's, mom's, sister's, and my handprint on each side of the box. As I noticed the prints while running by, I immediately hoped that my sister and mother would be safe and ready to go when I arrived at our boat. Coming to the back door of our house I stood there thinking I would never see this home again. I saw out of the corner of my eye a necklace that always hung on a hook near our back door. This necklace was the same necklace that my dad gave to my mother to ask her to marry him. We always had it hanging near the back door as was tradition in our world of ZAZRI among the Gri. This was done to remind whoever was leaving the house secretly as "somebody else" we would remember who we really were and the family name we represented. Before we were going to shape shift into another life form, we would see the necklace and remember who we represent. Often this deterred us from doing something that we would regret.

I grabbed the necklace and opened the door and headed for the woods. The sun was just going down and there was limited light due to the Cluds ship that was over our planet blocking the rays. I knew the path to get to our boat, so I didn't need much light, but the temperatures had dropped significantly as well. I hadn't grabbed a coat, but because of the rush of what was happening on our planet I didn't feel cold personally. I looked at my arms as I reached the woods shortly after running out my back door and saw some goosebumps all over, but I thought nothing of it. I could hear loud screeching like a dying whale which I knew was coming from the Clud. They were a very dangerous race that were always seeking to ravish other planets and live off the labors of others. I could also hear other Gri yelling and screaming as they were in commotion with the Clud invasion. This propelled me to run faster and not look back as I entered the woods. The further I ran the less and less I could hear anything other than my own breathing and thoughts.

After running for a couple of minutes I came to the bridge that connected our woodlands and the area where our boat was being stored. I hoped my mother and sister were already there waiting for me. As I was about to leave the woods and cross the bridge, I heard the voices of some Clud talking in Clud. This was a language that I was very unfamiliar with, but anyone would recognize it because it was different than any other language. They would hiss and cough at the same time and the frequencies and duration of their hisses or coughs would differentiate what they were saying. Their coughing was sort of a clearing of the throat. Both the hiss and the cough were very deep and detectable as Clud. I stopped running just before leaving the thick of the woodlands. I hid right behind a big peach tree that was just beginning to produce ripe fruit ready for picking. I took a glance up and saw a group of peaches right next to each other and they looked so juicy, but I had no appetite at that moment. I peeked around the tree hoping to see the Clud, while trying to control my breathing after running so I wouldn't get noticed by my loud respiration.

As I caught my breath, I realized that the Clud weren't paying attention to the forest where I was hiding, and I got the idea that I could still make it to my boat without getting caught if I went under the bridge. As the Clud continued talking I saw an opportunity to leave the woods and go down towards the marshlands under the bridge. As I began to slowly cross the marshes underneath, birds began to chirp and fly upward above the bridge. As I realized what was happening, I quickly looked for cover behind a bigger bush that was right in front of me. I ducked under it and tried to be as still as possible. I heard the Clud's voices a little clearer now than before as a few of them poked their heads over the bridge and looked down at the marsh. I'm hoping the birds will calm down soon and stop chirping so the Clud will not inspect anything further under the bridge. Feeling completely powerless, I cleaved to the necklace to try to find the strength and courage to be patient and hope that I wouldn't get discovered. I was trying to think of what I would do if I was found by the Clud. I had thoughts of my father who sacrificed himself so willingly to allow me to flee after the initial invasion of the Clud on Zazri. I began thinking of what my mother and sister would do if I didn't make it to the boat. After nearly having a panic attack, the birds finally calmed down after a couple minutes, which seemed like forever. I hoped that with the birds calming down the Clud would lose their interest in the marshes below them. Almost immediately after the birds stoped chirping, I heard the Clud's voices fading, and I thought it would be safe to slowly turn my body around to see if I could see any Clud still looking down. Thankfully there wasn't a Clud in sight and I felt so relieved. Continuing forward across the marshes I made sure to go slow and avoid stepping on anything that would make a lot of unnatural noises. I tried to keep my head on a swivel between the bridge and my next step. I didn't want a Clud randomly poking its head over and discovering me. I knew that going slow would take longer, but I'd rather make it to the boat late and in one piece than not make it at all. I figured if my mother and sister were there waiting, they wouldn't leave until it was too late. There was still time before they would need to leave. Making my way through the marshes I saw the birds flying above the bridge and I thought that they would cause the Clud to do a more extensive search under the bridge if they started chirping again. I was looking for another place to hide when I noticed that the birds were just flying in circles without chirping and they didn't look like they were going to give me away, thankfully. Finally, after making it through the marshes, I made my way up the hill under the bridge to make sure I wouldn't get noticed by the Clud. I sneakily lifted my head just high enough to where I could see above the railing of the bridge to get a better view of where the Clud were. I felt like a predator sneaking up on some prey, as I could barely get an eye high enough to see without being noticed.

The Clud are terrifying in every way shape and form. They were large, mostly black figures with 4 appendages from their main body. They all have a long curvy horn protruding from the back of their head that curves parallel with the neck and points out away from the shoulders. This protects their neck from the back and can cause serious damage if they were to head butt somebody or something from the back. They usually use it to break things down and would prefer to use their body weight to bring down an individual and bite at it as if it were falling on someone. The Clud differ in their appendages, however. The Clud were distinguished by the number of legs they would have. The more intelligent and evolved Clud had only two legs like a human and the less intelligent and evolved Clud had four legs. They had what would look like two separate mouths. This was because their lips didn't connect in the middle, as if the lips weren't continuous on the top or the bottom. There was a big, sharp pointed tooth sticking out of the top, pointing downwards going about an inch below the bottom the lip when the mouth was closed. The rest of the teeth in the mouth were similar with the bigger teeth on top and the smaller but still equally sharp and pointy on the bottom. With the mouth open as wide as it could go it'd be able to put five whole oranges in its mouth. The neck was very stout. Starting at the bottom of the neck from the shoulders down towards their main body were all covered in scales with a thick red line down the middle of each scale. The Clud's legs were thick skinned and black with a red line down the outside of each leg going from the heel to the top of the leg just before it connected to the scaley part of their main body. The Clud with arms had similar features as their legs with the same thick skin and a line running along the outside of the arm down to the outside of their last finger. They only had 3 long looking fingers with a big claw at the end which would cut right through any Gri flesh without any resistance. Their claws re-grow after four days of losing a claw. For their feet they have two large strong fingers with claws in front and one short finger in the back. The Clud need their back toe to keep their balance and essentially stay alive. Legend has it that the Clud who lose one of the toes that point backwards will be eaten by the other Clud. They can't regrow that toe and they are seen as weak so the other Clud prey on them. Clud's need to eat flesh and meat to survive. A Clud can eat twice their body weight in a week's time. They will kill anything living that will provide them sustenance. The only thing other than flesh that they eat is a root grown from the Black Flower. These flowers flourish on most planets, especially in areas with little sunlight and warmth. Their roots are only about 3 inches long and the flower itself is two inches tall but has a very wide top. The pedals are black with a red line down the middle of them. The pedals are pointy on the outside and get bigger as they connect to the middle of the flower that connects the top with the stem. There is a red line down the stem that goes to the end of the root. There is a chemical reaction that happens between the root and the red substance that will create an egg in the stomach of a Clud as it interacts with the stomach. After the seed grows big enough to where it has a shell around it the Clud vomit it out. They then place the egg in mud which creates a perfect environ-ment for the seed to grow in the egg. The Clud won't hatch until the egg is about 6 feet long. The Clud that are produced this way always have 4 legs and come out fully grown and mature. The food they eat only helps them maintain their health, but it does not allow them to evolve or get bigger. Only the Clud with 4 legs will eat the Black Flower and only they can procreate. The Clud with two legs can only come from certain life forms inhaling too much ash. This type of transformation is very uncommon because you must inhale a lot of ash from a volcano that erupts on a planet with little sunlight, so the Black Flower is present.

Seeing that the Clud were all located near the middle of the bridge or at the other end I thought it would be safe to continue trekking towards the river. I always remembered going over this bridge with my family growing up on our way to our boat and knew that I was close. I stayed low but with haste ran towards the river where our boat was. Arriving at our boat I noticed that neither my mom nor my sister were there. "Where could they be?" I thought. "What if the Clud had caught them? Would I be able to make it on my own?" All these questions began racing in my head. I was very unsteady, and my body started to shake a little. I couldn't control my hands. I was so scared and all that was going through my mind was the worst-case scenarios. It was hard to be optimistic in a situation like this and anything positive just didn't seem to be plausible. I tried to calm myself down as I clung to the necklace. I decided that if there was still a chance for my family to make it, we would still need to clear away the debris off our boat. Beginning at the back of the boat I grabbed all the branches and leaves and tossed them over into the river. The propeller was completely covered with branches, and it wouldn't be very effective unless I cleared it out. Getting on my stomach and reaching downwards with my hand to move the branches so our boat would work I heard some twigs breaking behind me. I quickly turned hoping to find my mom and sister, but I saw my friend Macrill. He lived just a few doors down from me and was the same age. It was comforting to know that it wasn't the Clud there, but I still had hoped it was my mother and sister. As he got closer, I noticed he was covered in blood, but I didn't see any lacerations on him.

"Macrill, are you okay? What happened?"

"It all happened so fast. I was there with my parents when they pushed me out of the way as a Clud pounced on them. I was shocked and I couldn't move until my cousin Vrin grabbed me and pulled me behind a pillar outside our front porch. I saw my father die right in front of me just a couple feet away. I was completely powerless, and I felt I should have just died with him instead of being pushed out of the way. Vrin asked me where we could go to get away and the only place that came to mind was your boat by the river. On our way over we were discovered by the Clud and Vrin knew that we wouldn't make it, so she pushed me down a hill in the forest. Vrin was taken down by a Clud and got a good bite in her arm. After biting off most of her shoulder and bicep the Clud stopped attacking her for whatever reason. Just as quickly as it overtook her it had left. I didn't know why, but it did. Vrin's arm was hanging on by a thread and she and I both knew she wouldn't make it. She told me to leave and if I ever saw her family to tell them what happened and that she loved them. I am only here because my parents pushed me out of the way when the Clud first came for us and because she did the same."

I was speechless. I couldn't imagine seeing my parents and a cousin go through what they went through. Grabbing his arm and pulling him in, we embraced each other tightly and both began to whimper. Finally getting a hold of ourselves and knowing that we would need to get out of the river to give ourselves a chance at survival we began clearing away the rest of the debris. I went back to the back towards the propeller again and finished clearing away the branches. It wasn't much longer when I had come up to the boat that was now covered in debris and branches because we hadn't used it in a while. The boat was still dirty, but at least it looked better and usable compared to when I first encountered it. I went to the lock box next to our boat's gear box looking for the keys to the boat. The lock box was super dusty and pretty damp because of the rain and water that had leaked into it over the years. The key was near the back underneath some soggy papers that just ripped as I moved them away.

"Fingers crossed, let's hope it still works," I said. Macrill gave me a concerned look but tried to show optimism in his facial expression. Putting the key in with one hand and still clutching onto our family's necklace, I turned the key. Bop, bop, bop. the engine started. What relief came when we heard the engine working. I was hoping that the noise wasn't too loud to draw attention to any Clud that were on the bridge. I had no idea how much gas was in the boat, and I would have no idea how far we could go without it running out. I turned it off knowing that it would work when we needed it to. Macrill asked me what the plan was and why we hadn't left yet to get away from the Clud. After telling him that we were waiting for my mom and sister he didn't seem too optimistic about them being alive still. He tried to talk me out of waiting, but I wouldn't listen. I told him that we would head to the nearby city of Keensby. We had a ship there that was also hidden. We would take the ship to Ooba. We had provisions on the ship for our journey. The Clud would have difficulty finding the ship because it was on the edge of the city right by the river where there were few Gri living. They wouldn't make it that way while there were still plenty of Gri downtown. We would only be on our boat for about 20 minutes before we would arrive at our ship. For us to make it out of Zazri we would need to be there a half hour before sunset to give us enough time to take off without problems big enough that would prevent us from leaving. The longer we waited the more dangerous it would become for us, and our chances of survival would drastically decline. We still had an hour before sunset so we would have to leave in 10 minutes. This didn't give us much time, but we were both so worried about being seen by a ship flying above or if the Clud randomly came looking by the river.

Waiting those ten minutes felt like the longest 10 minutes of our lives. Everything was ready and the path was cleared for us to head to our ship, but even with all of that we had to wait. I would not leave this planet without the rest of my family. I had already lost my father and I was not going to lose my mother and sister as well. I was willing to wait till the last moment possible before it was too late. They never showed up and it was time to leave. I knew that we would have to leave and if we didn't then Macrill's chances of dying would be on my hands. Sadly, I started up the boat and Macrill unhitched the ropes and latches to the dock, and we started to pull forward. As we were almost to the middle of the river, we heard some yells coming from back by the dock. Turning around towards the yells, I saw my mother and sister running towards the dock frantically. I was so relieved to see them and immediately turned around to go back to pick them up. I noticed that they were being chased by some Clud that probably came from the bridge. I had so many questions about how they got there and why they were just arriving, but I knew those questions would have to wait. I didn't have time to think about how or why and instinctively I headed towards them. I noticed my sister was limping. She was putting her weight on my mother who had her arm under my sister's arm and around the back to better hold her. We were about 20 yards away from the shore when I saw that my sister's left leg was bloody. I thought that she had been attacked by a Clud and somehow got away which doesn't make any sense. They started making their way into the river and we met them just as the river was up to their knees. There were only two Clud chasing them, and they were 100 feet behind them. Macrill helped my sister in first and then they both pulled my mother up as I was screaming for them to hurry. As soon as they were both in, I put the boat into reverse hoping that we wouldn't be stuck far into the bank of the river. The Clud were about 40 feet away now and we were stuck. My mother and sister were both screaming as was Macrill. They both Clud jumped towards the boat when they were about 15 feet away.

Zu Zu

Suddenly both the Clud were unconscious, and their bodies plopped over on our boat. Their back half didn't make it all the way into the boat, but their front legs and head were draped over our boat. I turned towards where the noise came from and saw two men standing in a boat with their rifles pointed toward the Clud. They had two more women in their boat as well and I supposed that they were their wives. The only thing I could do was smile faintly. I didn't have enough energy to give a full smile. I was very shocked at what had happened. My mother turned and said the most genuine thank you I have ever heard. We knew that we would all be dead if it were not for the two men with rifles. I wondered where they had come from but didn't have time to ask.

"Y'all better get out of here." Said the man on the right who looked a little older and had a beard. Then they waved and drove down the river in the opposite direction of where we were headed.

Macrill jumped out and started to push the boat out towards the middle of the river and I kept the engines in reverse. We were now on our way towards our ship, and we all hoped that it wouldn't be too late. We knew that as it got later not only would the Clud be able to see better, but from what we know about the Clud they usually invade planets in two separate groups. The second one always comes right at sunset meaning that the sky would be full of Clud ships. I stayed at the wheel and my mom and sister came over and we gave each other a big hug. During our ride they told me what had happened to them and why they were so late in getting to the boat. My mother told me what happened to my sister as she was bandaging up her leg to stop the bleeding. She tripped on a rock and hit a big branch right above the knee which cut her pretty good. I guess that was better than getting attacked by the Clud assuming that not many people escape the Clud after getting attacked.

We figured out our plan once we were to arrive at our ship to give us the best chance of survival. Seeing where we had our ship stashed away, we turned the boat engine down so it wouldn't draw as much attention to the noise. Keensby was a bigger city and we supposed that he Clud would attack here first because there would be more Gri to eat. We were still on the edge of the city, but we didn't want to take any chance of being noticed. We pulled up next to our ship that was covered by a large tree. All the trees were large so it didn't stand out from any others, but we had put a big gash on the side facing the river with an ax so we would recognize it. For as long as I can remember we have had our ship there.

Quietly, but quickly we jumped off the boat without even anchoring it down to anything so it wouldn't float away. My mother had the key to the ship and went to unlock it with my sister, while Macrill and I started removing some branches and brushes from around the ship. The ship wasn't any bigger than our boat, but it's all we needed to make it off Zazri. It was bright blue with a big half dome shaped out of glass over the top. I was surprised to see the paint job still intact considering how little we had used it recently. Macrill moved those branches off the glass. Once we were about to head onto our ship it turned on. The ship immediately lifted off the ground without going anywhere and the lights inside turned on. We ran inside and closed the door behind us. My sister was already seated, and my mother punched the ship into take off as soon as she knew that we were on. I sat right behind my mother and as we were leaving, I put the necklace around her neck. Though I couldn't see it I thought that she was smiling after realizing that we still had the necklace.

Keep your eyes peeled for Clud. We still have a couple minutes before we leave the atmosphere and can use the hyper speed. Whoom. A laser went right by our ship just before we were outside of the atmosphere. We kept gunning it as fast as we could go, and it appeared that the Clud ship that had fired at us was increasing its distance between us. Moments later we were out of the atmosphere and my mom put it into hyper speed which takes a second to work. I could feel the ship about to lurch forward. "We made it." I thought.

BOP.

"Skade! Skade get up!"

"Macrill, what is it?"

"The Jubi are close."

Dakool

Being woken up abruptly is something that I will never get used to. Back on Zazri we would always sleep for hours on end and wake up when it was time, but never before. If anyone in my family ever woke up another while they were sleeping, they were considered the "bad guy". It's not that there could be good reason to wake up and there may be plenty of good reasons to wake up, but it's a disservice to the person sleeping to be woken up if they're still dreaming. Dreaming in my family was key to everything. It's how we knew what things we should pursue and in what trades we should spend our time. It helped us dictate when we should go do certain activities and when to reach out to others. A lot of the more important decisions in our life were made based off our dreams. Dreaming you could say was literally part of our family.

After sitting up, I rubbed my eyes a couple of times because they itched. They usually do itch after I dream. They didn't always itch, but ever since coming to Ooba they have always itched after dreaming for some reason that I've yet discovered. I have my theories. The most prominent one in my mind is that it is due to the lack of darkness on Ooba. You see Ooba is surrounded by not just one, but two stars. Both are very bright and always there. You can't hide from the light. In Jacoby you will never find darkness in the open, it's just not possible.

Jacoby is a smaller city compared to some other cities on the planet. It still has its fair share different races.

Another farfetched theory of mine is that our eyes itch because we live in such close proximity to the Jubi. Jubi are a dominant race here on Ooba which makes sense considering they created it. They are these big looking creatures that smell horrendous. They are, well, they just smell really, really, bad. I think that they emit this poison that messes with our eyes.

The water we drink isn't all natural either, which causes some chemical reactions with our eyes as well. You see Ooba has some small reserves of water in every city, but it's a mixture that isn't normal. The water is brought in from neighboring planets which are good and normal on the other planets, but the Jubi think differently, so they try to make it "good" again by adding a bunch of chemicals to make it drinkable again. And they say they're the smart ones. Sometimes I don't think they're too smart.

"Okay Macrill. I'm up you can stop patting me on the back now." He nodded and got off the couch. I knew we had our door locked, but I was uneasy. A drop of sweat started to clump at the bottom of my nose. Heading towards the mirror in the other room my faint hopes faded. If we were caught, I was going to die for sure. My eyes were "ripped" as they called them here. Ripped was this idea of your actual eyes appearing like they have big cracks in them like a desert floor would look like when it was dry. They appear super brown all around the pupil which changes to a light-yellow color. "My eyes are so ripped." I thought. This always happens to people who just wake up from sleeping. It usually doesn't wear out for 10 minutes. If you get caught like this, you're as good as dead.

"Macrill. We good to go through the back if needed?"

"Let me check" responded Macrill. This better not turn south I thought. I knew if I were caught then Macrill would have to tell my mother that I was a dead man.

Looking out the window I saw the Jubi walking off down the road in the distance. A calm feeling passed over me. It still wasn't safe for me to go out until my eyes returned to normal to avoid any detection by others. Macrill and I got talking about the old days on Zazri before the Clud. He asked about my dream, but I wasn't ready to talk about it yet and my eyes went back to normal.

"Let's head back, shall we?" Macrill understood that I didn't want to talk about it at the moment, so we started to make our way out of the house and back towards Jacoby.

On our way back to Jacoby we saw young Jubi kids playing around. They looked like they were having a lot of fun. There were just two of them and neither of them were older than 8 years of age. Yet they were both bigger than Macrill and I. Jubi are an interesting looking race. They have a fish-looking head with a normal looking body that is grey. They are very muscular looking in their upper half where their chest, stomach, and arms are. Their skin is very tough and grey. Their legs are strong, but they don't look very coordinated. They have suctioned feet. And the most insane thing happens when they think of something. It can become tangible in their hands. The objects just appear in their hands whenever they think of it.

As we walked by the kids, they didn't seem to pay us any attention as they were too busy having fun.

The city of Jacoby was full of very tall buildings. The bottom third of all the buildings were where the people lived. Most people usually don't leave their buildings because they work there and have their quarters there. The bottom third of all the buildings is always very wide compared to the upper two thirds of the rest of the building. The houses have shared walls. Every house has a balcony, so they have access to the outside. Some houses have plain colors like all black or all blue while others have random household items draped all over the banister. Others have lots of pets freely roaming on their balcony all day every day. Some have lots of tools and pieces of hardware. Usually, their houses are decorated in a way to help them remember their past homes.

The biggest building was in the center of the city. The building still looked like the other buildings with houses on the bottom third, but it was just a lot taller than the other buildings. This is where the government officials would have their meetings and make decisions that they thought were best for the people of Ooba. There were multiple branches of the government all serving different purposes to ensure Ooba's prosperity. Some branches worked mainly with security and trying to keep the peace through physical demands. These workers consisted of a lot of Lexlands. Lexlands or Lex as they were often called came from Lexly. They are robotic in their appearance. About 85 percent of their makeup is metal. Their brains are fully functional and very human looking. They also have two fingers on each of their hands that have pink looking flesh. Instead of having hands they just have two fingers that protrude out of the bottom of their metal wrists. You always have to be careful around their fingers. They have this ability to shrink or enlarge anything that they touch with their fingers. Their heads are your typical square shaped with two big eyes in the front. They don't have a nose or ears, but they can hear which I've yet to figure out. They are very smart and logical and don't make many mistakes.

Then we have the branch that helps those in need. They provide jobs for people and help the economy to be sustainable. Jubi work in this department for the most part. I find it ironic because the Jubi are the hardest working race I know of, yet so many Jubi's seem to always need help. We also have part of the government who oversees the other branches called the Top branch. They usually make decisions regarding certain laws that should be enacted or enforced. Also, 80 percent of their employees are Jubi.

There are few Gri that work in the government. Us Gri don't always like working with others for extended periods of time. We often get upset and frustrated easy and then we like to take our anger out on people. I think it's best that there aren't a lot of Gri in the government.

I live in the building just North of the governmental building. Our building is one of the smallest in the city. Unlike most buildings we're missing about two thirds of our building. We only live there, but we don't work there. The people in our building oversee maintaining the natural and unnatural aspects of Ooba. This usually means we go out of the city most days and nourish and treat the surrounding ecosystems around Jacoby. I think I would go crazy if I had any other job than this one. I couldn't stand staying in the same building all day every day and rarely go outside.

Considering there are two suns around Ooba it is very hot outside. I would still prefer wearing protective gear than never going outside except for a little bit at the end of your workday. Working with my hands alongside my buddy Macrill also has its benefits. We usually find a way to have fun and make our work a little more enjoyable. Well, we don't always "work" as some think we do. Often, we go out on our own and goof around. Sometimes we get into mischief. We have a good time. We try to not take our job so seriously because we tell ourselves that we will get overwhelmed, so it helps us by having a little fun.

After saying bye to Macrill as he went up another flight of stairs to his place, I entered my house. I heard the necklace make a beating noise as it hit the door when I swung it open. Our house wasn't anything special and it was by no means big. Only my mother and I lived here, and we were hardly ever here at the same time. My sister had gone missing a while back after some weird instances had come up. My mother was probably at work in the forest right now. I grabbed an orange out of the basket on our table and started to peel it. I headed outside to our balcony to sit down and enjoy my orange outside. Just as I sat down, I noticed some Lexlands dressed in government uniforms heading towards our building. "This can't be good." I thought. Usually if the Lexlands are coming in your direction it's not a good sign. I immediately thought about the dream I had earlier that day and thought that maybe somehow, they had found out about it. I didn't know what to do. I just thought I'd have to act normal and deny anything that could get me into custody. I was on the second floor, and I didn't hear any noise coming from the stairs, so I thought maybe they were here for somebody else. I poked my head outside the balcony to see if I could see the Lexlands leave, but nobody left our building. There were sounds of footsteps coming from the stairs. They were on my level now. "What were they wanting or looking for?" I thought, hopeful that it didn't have anything to do with me.

Knock, Knock

"One second" I said wearily. I stood there for a second sweating but trying to keep it together to answer the door. I slowly pulled the door back and gave a faint smile, "Hello." I said taking a big gulp. There were two Lex standing there much bigger than I was and both looked very intimidating. Their fingers were down by their sides, but if I wasn't scared before, I was now. Their fingers scared me, knowing what they could do.

"Were looking for information about the shortage of food in the reserves that are found in the forest." He said in a deep, clear voice, "Do you know anything about this?"

"No, um no." I said, trying to sound confident. "I haven't heard about any shortage of food in our reserves. This is the first-time hearing about it." I was relieved that they were worrying about something that this time I really wasn't guilty of. They both just stared at me for a second.

"Have a good one sir" the other Lex said to me. I closed the door. I could feel my heartbeat drop drastically. I thought of Macrill and hoped that he would be okay. Thoughts of my mother also came racing into my mind. Once the Lexlands had left our building I would have to go to her. After an hour passed, I heard some steps coming down the stairs and continuing down. I went to my balcony to see them leave. They left and there wasn't anybody with them. I wondered if they found out what happened to the reserves, but as long as I had food, I didn't worry too much about it. "It wasn't my problem." I thought. I quickly ran upstairs to talk to Macrill. On the way up I just about knocked down a man coming down the stairs. It was Macrill. I was so relieved to see him. We embraced each other. After talking about our little experiences with the Lex I mentioned I had to go check on my mother in the forest. He thought it wasn't too smart, but I wasn't going to listen to him.

"She's probably just fine" he said hoping to deter me from leaving.

"I have to see for myself." You see, other than Macrill all I had was my mother. My dad, well yeah, my dad and my sister were no longer a part of the picture. "I can't lose my mom too." I thought. I had a bad feeling that maybe something had happened, so I bolted out of the building to go in search of my mom.

On my way out I happened to get a quick glance at the government building. I felt as if somebody were watching me from above. I turned my head to get a quick glance and there he was. "Dakool" I thought. He was on the first level balcony above the house level. The first level after the houses was the security branches level. There he was, looking down at me intently from the government building. I tried to look normal, but I'm sure he could see right through me. "Mom" I thought, as I ran off towards the forest.

It occurred to me that everything I was doing looked suspicious. I had no idea what had happened to the reserves of food that were now missing, but it would make sense why they would want to question me further on the matter. Working out in the forest and with the food missing from that area gives the Lex plenty of reason to at least approach me about the matter. Now Dakool himself, the leader of the security department, has just spotted me running towards the forest, just after my building was questioned on the subject. My sister had gotten into some trouble with them before so he could easily assume that I was a prime suspect. Regardless of all of this I had to get to my mom and make sure she was okay. There was also a special warmth I got whenever I was around her. After my recent experience I needed that feeling.

My mother could be anywhere in the forest working. Not knowing where to look first I started asking the workers that were at the edge of the forest to see if they knew where my mother was. One of them pointed me in the direction of where he thought he saw her. "Thank you." I said hastily. After heading in the direction, I was pointed to, I saw her. She was calmly pruning a tree in a group with three others. Usually, we were supposed to work in groups of 4 just to help morale because our work can be demanding. Obviously, that's why Macrill and I just leave our group and do our own thing.

"Mom." I shouted, a little ways off. Running towards her, I saw her face had a concerning look. She could always tell when something was wrong or wasn't right. I ran into her arms and gave her a big hug. Relieved that she was okay. I caught my breath and then told her what had happened with the Lex. I mentioned that Dakool had also been watching me as I headed out towards the forest in search of her. Just as I finished telling her the story, she and the others she was with all began to show a little concern in their faces. BAAAAAH, BAAAAAH, the sirens went off. That meant that the workers were to head back to the office on the edge of the forest. We were only about 50 yards away from the office when we saw the Lex in government uniforms approaching. "Mom," I said. "Dakool is with them".

Trouble in Jacoby

Good thing I was still in my protective suit. If I had taken off my protective suit, then I would have fried. Here on Ooba, we must wear these protective suits to keep us from heating up from the two suns that revolve around Ooba. These suits come in all different sizes and colors to fit everyone. The protective suits are comfortable. They have a protective silky layer on the outside that helps absorb the heat then it's funneled towards the back of the suit where it gets emitted out of the suit again. The underlayer of the suit is made of a substance only found on Ooba called Fuz. It's taken from the forest leaves. The fuz acts as a cooling agent to prevent the individual in the suit from heating up. If someone is caught outside without their suit, they won't last longer than 6 hours before they die. The exposed part of the body will start to bubble and turn purple. They will have a hard time concentrating and their sight will start to fade. So, it was a good thing I had my suit on still.

"Skade," my mother said as we were about 20 yards away from the workers office, "You need to get back to the house." "No." I said, trying to sound firm and positive. "I need to see for myself what this is all about." You see we almost never get called back to the office once we're already working in the forest or the fields or hills. Last time we got called in was a couple of years ago because there was a big earthquake on the southside of the city, so everyone was sent home.

Reluctantly I sided with my mother. I started to head back to my house when I had the idea to hide near the edge of the building by some small bushes. I needed to hear for myself what this was all about. It had to be very serious if they were calling the workers in and Dakool was with the security force.

"We have called you here today to discuss some recent events that took place in the food reserves building in the forest." Said Dakool with a straight, serious face. He went on to talk about how some food had been missing and how a Jubi was murdered and a Gri was found with ripped eyes. Basically, their eyes were dry and brownish yellow. It is caused when people close their eyes for an extended period of time. It's usually considered that the person with ripped eyes was sleeping and probably dreaming. Both bad, but especially dreaming.

They had taken the Gri into custody, but he was not the killer. They still have him in custody, and he will probably receive some life sentence or some torture routine. I was shocked when I heard that. Ever since the Clud attacked Zazri and other planets in the universe there has been less fighting. Probably because a lot of people lost close ones to the Clud's raids and are sick of fighting and seeing people lose close ones. It still happens, but not nearly as frequently so it always comes as a shock when something as serious as a murder happens.

Whoever was the person that got caught sleeping was in for some serious trouble. Usually if people sleep, they can get off a little easier, but if they find that they were dreaming then there'd be no hope.

Dakool went on to mention that there was a reward for the person who had killed the Jubi. The reward was hefty. He then asked if anyone knew anything about the killing or the missing food and that's when I left. I had to go back a different way than normal to avoid being seen out of place by the Lex officials. It took me a little longer to get back to the city, but as I was approaching, I could hear what sounded like people yelling. As I got closer, I saw some Jubi arguing with some Krimps on one side of the street. On the other side there were some more Jubi who looked like they were about to come to fists with some Lexlands. Behind them were some Gri who looked like they wanted to get in on the action as they started to approach the Lexlands and the Jubi. I noticed something flying in my direction and instinctively ducked. CRACK. A big blue bottle had just cracked on the road right next to me. I looked in the direction of where the bottle came from and saw a Jubi creating another bottle in his hands and was about to throw it in my direction again. I took off. The closer I got to the center of the city the less violent it was. I saw a couple groups of Lexland officials gathering and trying to herd people back to their houses. I thought they should go to the outskirts of the city where there were actual disturbances, but I just kept on my way trying to avoid any trouble or confrontation. My building was in sight now and I thought I saw Macrill standing out on his balcony as if he were waiting for something to happen. As I got closer, I could pick out his facial expression, it was a very distressed look as if he'd gotten fired or caught for doing something dumb. I had no idea beforehand that he had found out the details of what was happening in the city because of the death of a Jubi.

I ran inside and headed upstairs towards his place. He was holding the door open waiting for me as I came out the stair door. "What happened?" I asked him innocently.

"What happened?" He responded in a way that made me feel dumb for asking him. "What happened? Why don't you tell me what happened?" I recounted to him about finding my mom and how the sirens went off and Dakool came and spilled some light. There was a reward for the killer and there was a Gri who was sleeping and possibly dreaming. Just the main details of what had happened in the forest. He didn't know about any of that. He only saw that there were some littles scuffs in some parts of the city and people were becoming violent for some reason. He figured people wouldn't get that upset if they found out some food was missing so he figured something else had to be going on.

I guess the Government had issued a statement alerting all the people of Jacoby of the incident and now they were turning towards violence. After seeing the statement Macrill went to the balcony to see if he could see anything happening, but he told me nothing had happened in or near our building. He was still a little taken aback though at the news. As was I. Still trying to process everything I had heard and seen the last couple of hours or so I needed some food and some rest.

Getting some rest was normal back on Zazri, but since our arrival on Ooba we've accustomed ourselves to being able to live without the need for sleep. I still had my old tendencies clearly.

Macrill knew better than to let me fall asleep in our building let alone in his room. He could get in trouble if I fell asleep in his house. Macrill had adapted better than I had, and he never needed to sleep.

I laid down and Macrill gave me some crackers with some oranges to eat. Slowly nibbling on the food, I began to close my eyes, but every 20 seconds I would hear Macrill, "Don't even think about it." I got a little rest, knowing deep down that I wanted to sleep so bad, but I knew there was too much at stake if I did and somebody discovered us. After resting, without sleeping may I add, for two minutes or so and after talking with Macrill I decided it would be best to go back to my house downstairs, thinking that my mother probably got let go from work.

I walked down the stairs and opened the door to my house. Immediately I was overcome with feelings of confusion, disbelief, and helplessness. My mom was sitting on our couch with her hand and her head bleeding profusely. "What happened?" I asked my mother as I ran towards her. "Who did this?" I thought to myself as I got to her. Somebody was going to pay.

Trying to keep calm and collected as I was bandaging her up around her elbow and her chin was very difficult. My mom wouldn't tell me who did it. She claims that she "didn't remember" but I knew she was too nice to rat anybody out. You see my mom wasn't like most Gri. Most Gri get angry easily and almost always look to get even. We had this grumpy demeanor about us most of the time and if somebody so much as looked at us funny we'd think that they were not to be trusted. My mom though, was very different for some reason. She always seemed to be the peacemaker and was very calm in tough situations. Sometimes I wondered how I was her son.

She went on to tell me what Dakool had said, not knowing that I was secretly there listening to him as well. I acted very intrigued and taken back as if it was my first-time hearing about it. It was still crazy what happened, but I've already had a little time for it to sink in and process it. Later, on her way back after being released for the day, which was customary when something big like this occurred, she just remembers getting some help from the Lex officials.

"You going to be okay?" she asked me wearily.

"Yeah." I replied though I knew she could read right through me and knew better.

"Promise me," she said, "you won't go looking for trouble".

"Okay." I said hesitantly after a long sigh.

Just after our conversation we heard a loud explosion as if it were close. We quickly found out that it was too close. There was some smoke right outside our balcony that was rising from beneath us. Our building had been hit by a bomb. We quickly ran to the patio which probably wasn't the smartest thing to do looking back at it, but we wanted to see the damage for ourselves. We saw some Jubi running off across the street from us, so we figured they'd done this. They were probably blaming our building and the people that lived there for the murder of the Jubi. Thankfully the Lexlands office was right next door so just as soon as the bomb went off, we had about 15-20 Lex working on calming down the flames and seeing the people who needed medical attention. We went back inside after we couldn't breathe because of the smoke and caught our breath.

The city was in chaos, and it seemed to only be getting worse. Tension was rising amongst the different races. Violence was at an all-time high. We didn't know when things would calm down or if the murderer would even be caught. Within 20 minutes of the bombing of our building the government put out a new statement urging everyone to keep calm and not to resort to violence. They claimed that Jacoby was officially in a state of chaos. They were seeking help from nearby cities due to the recent incidents that had taken place. About 32 people had been sent to get medical help and luckily no fatalities. In the next 2 hours everyone was to go back to their homes and stay inside until given further notice that it was safe to leave.

This was my time I thought. I was going to get revenge on somebody for what happened to my mother. I knew I only had 2 hours to leave and come back. My mom went into her room and was resting on her couch. "Now or never" I said to myself quietly. I knew what I wanted to do. I quickly shape shifted into a Lex and headed for the door.

I Get Revenge

Sometimes it's hard to not act like myself when I shape shift. Shape shifting is a very simple concept and very common back on my home planet Zazri amongst the Gri. You see all Gri can shape shift. Like most things it has its drawbacks. There are certain limitations to shape shifting that we must work with. Whenever we shape shift, we always have to have one aspect of our physical appearance stay the same, something visible. We can choose what that part is, but for the most part we always keep our eyes. For whatever reason our eyes usually stay the same when we shift. This takes practice to be able to decide what stays the same. Early on, it's hard to control, but the more experienced shifters can do it just as easily and normally as they breathe. It has become second nature.

When I was young, I shifted into my friend, and I had my whole leg stay the same. It was very noticeable. You see he was 2 feet taller than me so you can only imagine I was very lopsided. Walking was tough. Running was completely out of the picture.

The longer we sustain the new form usually the longer it takes to recover when we shift back to our normal selves. This was easy to deal with back on Zazri because sleeping was okay there, but since coming to Ooba you don't notice too many people shape shifting. There are too many risks. The whole law that you can't sleep here complicates things. It's too great a risk to shape shift because you'll often fall asleep. Some Gri can do it, but it takes all their will power to not fall asleep after.

I've shifted a couple times here on Ooba, but I've always had my sister help keep me awake afterward. I haven't shifted for 7 months. That marks the time when my sister was taken by the Lex for some reason that I have never understood. My mom claims she doesn't know and refuses to talk about it. My mom has never shifted since arriving on Ooba as she says, "My shifting days are over." My mom always wanted to make things right here on Ooba and she's tried to indoctrinate me into adapting to the new culture with its laws and regulations. I don't agree with it, but I wouldn't tell her that knowing it would hurt her if I did.

Among other things with shifting, we can only shape shift into somebody that we have seen. We can only shift into the same gender. The more similar the characteristics the easier it is to maintain the shift, allowing us to stay in the new form for an extended period of time. Pretty simple idea, right? Just wait until you actually do it, and it feels like the most complex thing in the world. Trying to worry about portraying the person you shifted into correctly. Not acting like your normal self but having to change your whole demeanor and mannerism to match the new form. Thinking like the new person is something I don't think I will ever fully grasp, but I try. Hearing the way we talk and seeing our new parts once we shift is so bizarre. All our insides stay the same obviously shrinking or growing depending on the new size of the form we take. Seeing how our new form affects our strength and endurance. Our speed, the way it feels to walk, or run is different. Most things just feel a little off which is totally normal in shape shifting.

Outside was absolute chaos. People screaming and running in all directions. Random objects flying through the air. I had to duck right as I got outside because a rock the size of an orange flew right towards me. I didn't even look like a Gri, and a rock was being thrown at me. I guess Gris weren't the only ones being blamed for the murder. Running through the city bumping shoulders with people on my left and my right. Stopping every once in a while, when a big group was cutting in front of me. I could see Krimps naturally going a little faster than everyone around them.

This wasn't because the Krimps were naturally faster than others but because they can do this weird time freeze thing, so it looks like they are going faster than others. I saw a couple little push stores that had new decorations on them. I don't think the owners approved of the new decorations to their push stores. One had a bunch of paint all over it and the merchandise had been charred. The other one I saw had a wheel missing and glass was spread all over the top of the counter.

I didn't even know where I was going. I just kept running as if to blend in because that's what everyone was doing. I made my way about a mile out from my house where the crowd was smaller but no less chaotic. There was a group of Lex officials trying to detain some Jubi as some Gri were looking at them like they'd just offended them.

One of the buildings had caught fire and there were some Jubi and Krimps working together to put it out before it got any worse.

Then I saw it. My opportunity came that I knew I had to seize. There were some Gri standing on the corner by the burning build-ing. They didn't seem to be worried about the building on fire next to them. Just by the look of them I could tell that these Gri were a disgrace. Most races upon arriving here on Ooba adapt to the laws and rules, but they never forget about their culture. For whatever reason there was this small group of Gri that completely forgot everything about our culture and acted like completely different people. Thankfully there were only a small percentage of Gri that were like this. "These goons." I thought to myself. They're going to get what's coming to them.

Naturally I acted on the first thing that came to mind which was my first mistake. I grabbed a small rock that was right next to my foot and hurled it at one of them. Hitting one of them in the shoulder, he was taken off balance and fell to the ground. I didn't think I had that strong of an arm, but I guess it's different when you shape shift into a Lex that's super strong. The other 3 Gri that were with the guy that was now on the ground immediately had a look of shock on their faces, which quickly turned to anger. They looked around until they found me, which was the second dumb thing I did. I was just standing there looking right at them with this expression on my face that would make them look dumb if they thought anybody but me threw the rock. I was egging it on, and they were going to give it. For whatever reason, I didn't think that they would retaliate after one of them got hit by a rock. I also figured they'd be intimidated by my new look as a Lex, but it didn't seem to derail their idea to come after me.

Running desperately towards anywhere that would get me away from the approaching Gri, I weaved in and out of people. Bumping shoulders with others. Tripping over some bushes. Rocks flying past my head a little too fast for my likings. I knew they were coming from the Gri. I turned the corner to go down a different road hoping that they'd lose track of me. It was to little effect, and it seemed that they were gaining on me. Even with all the other Gri, Krimps, Jubi, and Lexlands around it didn't deter their efforts to get me. Just before reaching the end of the road to head into a building, I got hit from behind with a rock. My head jolted forward as I heard a rock hitting the ground right behind me after it pegged me in the head. Before I got to gather myself again to head into the building, two big hands with firm grips grabbed my arm, while two similar hands grabbed my other arm and lifted me up.

"What are we going to do to him?" said the Gri who was holding my left arm. WHAM. One of the Gri punched me right in the stomach. If the two Gri weren't holding me, I would have crumpled over because of the force. Just after that the fourth Gri, who was the one I hit with the rock, appeared, and held up the rock and was about to slam it against my head, but he stopped just before he did. It appeared as if he was looking at someone behind me who I couldn't see. There was something different about the Gri who was holding the rock though. One of his ears was a little bigger than the other. That wasn't normal. The left ear just didn't seem to fit with the rest of the body. It also had a cicatrix along the bottom of the ear as if it'd been cut through. It wasn't too thick, and you probably wouldn't notice it unless you were looking right at it. I thought maybe he had shifted from a different Gri into a new Gri. I was puzzled and surprised because you don't see too many shifters on Ooba. He looked at me as if he was going to get revenge one day, but his look quickly changed as he looked directly into my eyes as if he knew I was a shifter as well. Just as quickly as they had grabbed me, they were gone.

Rubbing my head with one hand and my stomach with the other hand, I turned to see who was there. It was a group of Lex. Luckily for me the building I was about to enter housed a lot of Lex. Once they saw me, they asked if I was okay and what that was all about. Before I could answer one of the Lex that appeared to be younger due to his smaller statue and size said, "What's wrong with his eyes". That's when I knew I needed to leave. I dashed off hoping that they wouldn't follow me. I figured I'd better get back to my house, I had gotten into enough trouble as it was.

As I returned towards my house there were a lot less people in the streets. This was probably because the end of the two-hour notice was about up before everyone had to be inside. With just minutes to go I made it to our building. Before I entered, I noticed a lot of Lex officials with different suits on than the ones from Jacoby. I figured they'd come from a neighboring city though I wasn't sure which. All of their suits were yellow, and it was hard to look at them. Probably would have blinded someone if they looked at them long enough. Their suits seemed a little more advanced than the ones we had so I figured they were made to last longer than 6 hours in the sun. I thought Jacoby would have the best stuff considering it was the biggest city on Ooba and the most populated, but I guess not.

I shifted back to myself after I realized nobody else was in the stairwell. It felt good to be normal again. I checked my stomach from when I was punched and sure enough it was bruised. It was still a little sensitive and it hurt if I put any pressure on it. Opening the door to our house ever so slowly as if that would not cause my mom to ask me questions about where I was. I was thinking what she was going to ask me and tell me about how worried she was. I poked my head through the door and quietly walked in. I didn't see my mom in our front room, and she wasn't out on the balcony either. I went to look in her room and she wasn't there either.

"Weird." I thought. I checked my room and nothing. Thoughts began to cross my mind one after another. "Where was she? Did she know I left and came after me? Did the Lex come and get her? Would she go to a neighbors?" All these questions seemed plausible at the time. The best option I thought was to ask Macrill. The government's notice didn't say anything about us needing to be in our houses, just not outside. I headed to Macrills house on the floor above mine.

Ring Ring.

"Macrill." I yelled.

A second later the door opened. It wasn't Macrill, but it was my mom. She looked better than when I left her two hours ago, but she still looked a little beat up and tired. "You promised me you wouldn't do anything." she said firmly. Then closed the door. So many feelings went through me in that moment. She was right. I promised her I wouldn't do anything, but I've never been good at keeping my promises and she knew that. I felt hurt and sad because my intentions were to make things right for her. My mom had never resented me before, so these feelings were so different and almost overwhelming. Some tears started to stream down my cheeks. I felt anger towards my mom. How could she resent me like this? Did she not want me anymore? Without even thinking about it, I headed back towards our house. I was going to run away.

I started to pack some stuff into my work backpack. I knew I wasn't supposed to be outside, but I'd rather face the Lex outside than deal with the disappointment from my mother inside. I was still very tired, which was normal after shifting. Especially in the heat of Ooba. Before I made it outside, I found myself sitting on our couch for what I thought would only be a minute to gather myself before I left. The last thing I remember was holding my backpack on my lap and looking outside our balcony window and then I closed my eyes.

My dream started with me running behind another Gri. I could only see his backside. It looked familiar, though I couldn't pinpoint exactly who he was or where I'd seen him before. There was something special about him though. I could hear some Clud behind us. Their screeches are very hard to forget once you've heard them before. They were a ways behind us, probably feeding on something because their sounds were fading as we ran. They could have caught us if they wanted to so that's why I assumed they were already having somebody else for dinner. "Whoa," I thought in my dream, "it was dark." We were on a completely different planet. It was never dark on Ooba because of the two stars that were always present. We seemed to be in a marshy place because it was wet. The clouds above us were dark and they looked like they would rain any second. The ground was full of mud and weeds. Thankfully, it wasn't too thick because we wouldn't make it far trying to run in thick mud.

I was getting tired. It seemed like we'd been running for 20 minutes which I was not in shape for. I turned around once or twice and only got a glimpse of a big city with multiple Clud ships just above the buildings. The bright red stripe that was apparent on all the Clud was also on the outsides of the ships. One big red stripe from the front of the ship going all the way to the back of the ship. The buildings looked different than the ones back in Jacoby and also on Ooba, so I didn't know where I was. The further we ran the more people I could hear running in the same direction as us on our left and our right. There came a point when we were so surrounded by trees that I couldn't see behind us or in front of us except for the next 5 feet. The darkness didn't help. I almost bumped into the person in front of me multiple times because he would slow down to duck under a branch or to take a quick side-step to the left or right to avoid running into a bush or a rock.

A light started to break through the trees. I could make out the silhouette of what looked like some small house connected to the trees hanging no less than 20 feet in the air. There seemed to be lots of them and some of them had big lights hanging underneath them. The closer we got to the lights the more people I saw. People were coming from all directions to this little village. They seemed to be running up to the tree which had some form of stairs spiraling around the base of the tree up towards the houses up above. Some trees had multiple houses on them. Those trees must have been strong. Other than the people and the trees the weather seemed to be the same. A little chilly especially after living on Ooba for the past 8 years. Damp forest floor. A little cold humidity. Still lots of trees and bushes everywhere, but they weren't as dense where the houses in the trees were located.

I continued to follow the other Gri up one of the trees. This tree was probably 22 feet in diameter. It was hard to pick out the color exactly even with the light shining on it from above. It looked light brown, and it was very rough to the touch. There were big cracks along the whole base of the tree. The steps seemed to protrude straight out of the tree forming natural steps. They were only about 2 feet wide, so you had to really watch your step going up.

I almost slipped off the stairs completely because they were so wet. Somebody from behind me grabbed my arm just before I fell off. "Uhh thanks" I said softly. The person just grunted back as if it were no big deal. I probably would have survived because we were only about 12 feet off the ground, but it still probably would have hurt.

The last step of the stairs was the floor of the house. There wasn't anything special about the house we had entered. Probably could fit 30 people in them is all if they were packed like sardines. The hut was perfectly square. The ceiling was about 15 feet above the floor. It was a tight fit for some of the Jubi that were with us. They were always bigger than the rest of the races. In the middle of the tree there were some more stairs that went upwards around the tree. There was a hole in the ceiling for people to go to the hut above.

"We have to warn the others." Said a voice inside the hut. I couldn't see who said it just because there were so many people in there. The voice was deep and scratchy as if his voice box had been broken or injured. I tried to squeeze around everyone to get a up close view of who was talking. After a couple failed attempts of maneuvering between and around people I decided to stop.

I couldn't seem to pick out exactly what was being said after the first comment. There was a lot of yelling and arguing with everyone in the hut. I did notice that there were a couple Gri and

Lex poking their heads down through the hole from the ceiling to listen in. I couldn't make out their faces, but you could see the shape of their heads with the contrast of the light coming in from above them.

"He's here" said a familiar voice softly. All voices shut off and everyone looked in the direction of where the voice came including mine. Everyone was looking at the Gri who I followed here. Because it was still so dark, I couldn't quite make out his face. Everyone stayed quiet and he said again, "He's here".

"What do you mean?" said somebody behind me closer to the corner of the hut, "Like here, here, on Porvenga?"

"He's right there." Said the Gri as he pointed in my direction. It was hard to tell exactly who or what he was pointing at until I realized everyone cleared a path for him to clearly point right at me. Luckily for me that's when I woke up, but unluckily for me I wasn't in my house on my couch where I remember being last. I didn't have time to process or think about my dream at that moment. I had other more important matters going on in real life. I was startled and confused. Then I realized.... This was the exact description of the prison house that I had heard some Jubi talk about long ago.

Goodbye

His dream went like this- Standing outside of a big house with both stars present in the sky. I could tell he was still on Ooba. This house was different though. Most houses were part of a big building close to a lot of other houses in the same building. This house was free standing, not connected to any other house or building. It was hot and his protective suit was off. His face was charred, and he looked like he was about to pass out. I could feel how he was feeling which was always so weird to me. He dropped to his knees and his eyes started to close just when the front door opened. A larger than normal Jubi came out of the door. He held out his hand and a cup appeared in his hand with some water. The water tasted so good. It was different than the normal water found on Ooba. The water was cool, and it sunk through my body with such a refreshing feeling. I felt strength surge through my body though I still needed to get inside. "Inside" he said. The Jubi grabbed his arm and put it around his shoulder as if he were lifting a little kid. Without saying anything he carried him towards his house. The inside of the house was full of toys and trinkets and random objects that were not found here on Ooba. He carried him deeper into his house as he pushed the things on the floor out of his way. He made sure he didn't trip or step on anything in his house. I was so confused as to why his house was so messy and full of random old objects that didn't look like they served any purpose. There were paintings hanging up all over the walls. The main room where the couch was, was so wide and open. One of the biggest rooms

I've seen in a house. There were 4 black pillars with bright red stripes down them, just like the Clud and their ships. There was a big hand mark with a J in the middle of it. "Don't worry," he said as if he could read my thoughts. But I was still a little concerned. There was something about his face that seemed a little cold and off. I didn't like this guy. "So," I said as he put me down on the couch to rest, "Why'd you do it?"

Then I felt a hand shaking me. "Whoa," I thought somebody was shaking me. I opened my eyes and saw on my shoulder two big fingers.

"The guards are coming." He said, trying not to sound suspicious, but there was nothing unsuspicious about it. I took my hand off Del's arm and went back to my corner.

Del was short for Deluther. His name was a little long to pronounce the whole thing, so everybody just calls him Del. Del was a Krimp. He was in here for robbing a couple stores. In the outside world he was one of the wealthiest people in Jacoby. He turned himself in because he wanted to change. Nobody would have been able to catch him or accuse him if he hadn't turned himself in. Because of this his sentence was reduced to 3 years instead of 25. He was always boasting about how much money he had had. "I made 45 Tez in one day." he would always say. Tez was the currency on Ooba. The people who worked in the fields usually only made about 3 Tez a day.

Our room was a 20x20 foot box. There was blue tape on the ground forming squares all around the floor to separate people. The room was cool, which was nice. We stayed there all day except for 2 hours when we got to leave the building under supervision to do some community service. They fed us 6 times a day. The meals weren't anything special. Most of the time it was the same food repeatedly. The room was all white except for the transparent glass wall at the front of the room. There were two transparent doors that were locked. They had a small little door that they would send the food through every 4 hours.

There were 8 of us in that one room. There were multiple other rooms throughout the jailhouse. Most of them were in for stealing some money or goods. A Lex was in here for shrinking his neighbor who then got trampled by his own family. Tragic story. And then I was in here for who knows what. I tried to ask the guards, but they never responded. My jail mates didn't know either, so I was left to assume that I was caught dreaming.

It had been a whole week since I could remember coming in here. The worst part about jail was when we had to leave and do some community service. We always did it right when the two stars were at their peak. It was so hot, and they claimed they didn't have any protective gear to give to us. We always came back a little sick due to the extreme exposure to the suns. We did random tasks in the city where everybody could see us. We got yelled at and heckled every time we went out. The guards always seemed to turn a blind eye when a group would come up and hassle us. Sometimes we'd come back with a bruised arm or a cut on our head apart from the blisters that would start to form on our skins.

The food we got in the prison wasn't too bad if you liked little bugs in it crawling around. Somehow, some of my cellmates liked the food.

A guard came up to the door, "Skade." he said, unenthusiastically. Taken aback, I wondered what he wanted me for. I'd been there for a week is all and I thought I had behaved good and didn't merit any extra form of punishment. I got up and followed him. I didn't know if I'd be returning, so I said bye to everyone as I left. I followed him down the hall and we passed a couple other rooms full of inmates. 8 people in each cell except one had 11 for some reason. They had me enter a room. The room was pretty small, and the guard closed the door behind me as I walked in. It was the only door in and out of this room. "Skade." Somewhere above me a familiar voice said. Hearing the voice was so calming, the first time I'd felt some sort of comfort in a long time.

Still confused at where the sound was coming from exactly, but I responded, "Yeah".

"It's your mother, Skade. It's me".

We chatted for a second catching up on what prison was like, our daily routines and the food. My mother was doing good other than being alone.

It was frustrating not being able to see her in person because that was better than just hearing her voice. The longer you stay in prison and the better you act there the more beneficial it becomes when you have visits. Since it was only the first week all I got was to hear my mother's voice. I guess you can say I was overjoyed to hear her voice again. I felt peace. I tried to sound positive and upbeat about prison and all, but really it was zero fun. We were basically trapped inside a room all day and it wasn't a big room considering the 8 other cell mates I had.

"Mother," I asked on a more serious note, "What happened? Why am I in here?" There was a long pause. I heard her take a deep breath. "The Lex came and did an inspection check and caught you sleeping."

Anger filled my whole body. I didn't appreciate how we couldn't dream, let alone sleep. I never understood the whole reasoning behind it all, but it made me so mad. "There's something else you should know Skade." she mentioned over the intercom quietly. "It's about your sister, she..."

BEEEP

A loud noise went off on the intercom and I didn't hear what else my mother was going to say. Our conversation was cut short. "MOTHER!" I yelled at the top of my lungs just as the guard opened the door and grabbed my arm and started to drag me back to my cell. I tried to resist, but it was useless. I was so little and weak compared to the Lexland.

Crying in my little boxed area in my cell, Del came over and asked me what had happened. I told him about my visit and how it was cut short. "Bad timing." he said sympathetically.

The food door opened and in came our food. I had no appetite to eat after what had just happened, so I gave my food to Del who I knew would eat it. All I could think about was what my mother was going to say about my sister. Last time I saw her was about 7 years ago. I don't know why, but she was taken by the Lex. I never saw her after that. I assumed it was because she was caught dreaming. Here on Ooba all dreamers who are caught are faced with severe punishment. I didn't have much time to think about it however because not long after the food came it was time to do some service out in the city.

It was hot. Since we didn't get any protective gear for ourselves while doing community service it was always miserable because of the heat. There was no escaping it either. Whatever direction you faced or turned one of the two stars was right there. They were so prominent and close it was inescapable.

Today we were working on the streets near the edge of the city. There was still some unrest and tension in the streets because of the incidents that had occurred over the past week or so. It was still good to get out even without a protective suit because it meant we could leave our little cell room. I recognized the street as soon as we arrived. This was the same area where I got into some trouble with the Gri. I didn't like being in this. I felt like I was being watched and they could easily pay the guards off to throw down some damage on me while we were out doing our clean up. There was trash and debris all over. Lots of the buildings had windows that were boarded up. There was glass all over. There were some Lexlands on the street that were just looking for trouble. They had that look in their faces that if anybody tried anything funny around them, they would pay. I tried not to make eye contact with them, though I knew they were looking right at us. I had a broom, and I began to sweep up some little dirt clumps and rocks that were on the side of the road. Del also had a broom and was helping me.

It was about mid-day which meant it was time for the work force transition period. Almost immediately there were hundreds of people walking through our street. Some were coming back from work while others were heading to work. People were coming in and out of the buildings we were working around. I saw a Krimp and a Jubi catching up on the other side of the street from where we were. I saw two other Gri hugging just before they went in different directions to work. There was a little scuffle right behind us near the entrance of one of the buildings. Del and I both backed up to not get involved. We kept our heads down so the guards wouldn't notice us as we weren't doing anything.

One Gri shoved another Gri right up against the building. He held up his fist like he was going to punch him, but he never did.

Suddenly a sense of worry came over me. The Gri who was being held up looked just like the one I'd thrown the rock at. His ear was different than the other, like before. "Hopefully he wouldn't notice me," I thought, as I turned the other direction in a way that I hoped wouldn't call attention to myself. Just as I did, the guards that were watching us went past me and headed towards the Gri. I heard the guards separating the Gri.

The streets were still crowded with people. I found it hard to focus on anyone specifically because there was just so much going on right in front of me. Then my eyes caught it from across the street in the building. A sign was held up that read STAY CLOSE TO DEL. Just as quickly as I saw it, it had disappeared. I tried to look to see who was holding it or where the sign had gone, but it was hopeless because I couldn't see clearly through all the people passing by. I kept sweeping because I didn't want to get caught doing nothing now that the little scuffle seemed to have cleared up behind me.

Del started sweeping again as well. The people finally started to clear up and the rush was over. There were maybe 10 or 15 other than Del and I out in the streets now. It had seemed so quiet compared to 10 seconds earlier. As we were sweeping, I leaned over to Del and told him what had just happened with the sign and if he knew anything about it. Just before he could answer though one of the guards called him over to the other side of the street to help move some bigger rocks. He didn't have a chance to answer my question, but as he walked off, he gave me a hopeful look as if he knew about the sign.

After cleaning up that street we cleaned up another street and the inside of a building that was burnt and trashed. The building seemed to be vacant. There were lots of Jubi working on it while we were cleaning up around their work.

We headed back to the jail house after finishing up at the building. We probably could have spent another 5 whole days there cleaning up, but we only got a certain amount of service hours a day and thankfully our time was up. I was exhausted, as were my mates.

We always had food delivered to us right when we got back from service because we all needed it. The water we had never tasted good, but it always tasted its best right after doing service without our protective suits. It felt so relieving to drink. Most of us saved a little water to put on our cell clothes to help cool us down.

Just after finishing our meal two guards came to the door and called me. They took me to a bigger room where there were 10 Lex officials or so. I was so stunned and confused at what was happening that I didn't get a good count.

There at the front of the room was a big chair with a smaller one on each side. I noticed who was sitting in the big chair. Dakool. "This can't be good". I thought to myself.

He gave me a sly and disappointed look as I walked in. I had never met Dakool personally, but his reputation was well known by everyone in Jacoby. He was probably well known in all of Ooba for all I know. He has been the best Lex official that Jacoby has ever seen. There's no deceit in him and he works harder than anybody to bring justice where justice is deserved.

Right after the incident that has caused so much violence in the city, I caught him looking at me as I was headed outside the city. I have never felt more guilty, and I hadn't even done anything.

"Skade", he said in a cool yet deep voice. I took in a big gulp. "This wasn't good." I thought. "We have found you guilty of sleeping," he said, then after a long pause, "and dreaming." Suddenly his eyes seemed to narrow in a little more on me than before. His gaze was so intense and penetrating. His face turned darker as if suddenly the two stars surrounding Ooba weren't enough to light up his face. I couldn't make eye contact with him for too long. I had to look away. I got a glimpse out of the corner of my eye, and it looked like the guards were smirking as if they knew I was going to pay heavily. As guilty as I felt in that moment, I still didn't regret the fact that I dreamed.

"We also find you guilty," Dakool went on to say, which caught me off guard. "Of the murder of Taple Vep" he continued.

"That's ridiculous!" I shouted. I was so surprised and confused. I don't remember what else happened because I almost passed out, probably from shock, but I think Dakool mentioned something about 2 days.

The guards basically carried me back to my cell. I don't remember much except feeling completely drained. I was so taken back that I didn't know what to think. "How could this happen to me?" I thought to myself. Surely Macrill would be able to tell them I was with him on the day of the murder. I couldn't have done it.

Del knew something was wrong because he came and put his arm around me. "Tell me everything." he said. There wasn't much to tell because I spaced out for a lot of it, but I told him the little that I remembered. He inhaled deeply. I could feel it as my head was against his chest.

That was a very bad hour. The food came in, but I was too depressed to eat. I had completely lost my appetite. I felt very sick. I had to go to the bathroom like every 10 minutes. My roomies were very sensitive to my circumstances and gave me plenty of space to take everything in. I felt bad for them because the toilet was in our cell, and it couldn't have been a pretty sight or smell with me using the toilet 5 times an hour.

"This was it." I thought. Might as well enjoy my time with my roomies who I'll never see again. We started playing some make believe games that we always played in our cell to help pass the time. Even the guards seemed to be a little more empathetic as they would walk by to do their checkups and they would give me a sorrowful look.

One of the guards called me over when he was doing his little check in. I drudgingly went to him. "You still get one more visit" he said quietly, as if hoping to cheer me up. I tried to hide the excitement and feeling of relief that came over me when he told me, but there was no reason to hide it. That cheered me up.

"Thanks." I said, though still trying to sound sad. I was looking for everyone to pity me which wasn't right, but I thought I deserved a little pity after what was going to happen to me. The guard left and I told Del that I'd get one more visit. He was so happy for me.

I found out that my visit would be tomorrow, which seemed impossible to wait that long, but I didn't have any choice. The day seemed to pass by extra slow and I couldn't get my mind off my mother. Does she know that I'm to be executed in two days? Does she have any idea what I'm feeling right now? These thoughts seemed to only make the day go by slower, so I tried focusing on other thoughts. The other thoughts were my fantasies of me living out the rest of my life on Zazri with my father and sister and mother. Macrill would be there too. We would be able to dream without any repercussions. We could live our lives out without any fear of the Clud. We wouldn't be afraid of shape shifting. We could just be ourselves and do what we do best. Then my thoughts turned towards some magical jailbreak. I knew that was a fantasy because nobody had ever escaped Dakool. That thought didn't last long. I was thinking of how we could go chill on the river and lakes in our old boat. We could cause a little mischief with our neighbors and not get in trouble for it. So many things that could be better than sitting in this cell with other random victims knowing that I would cease to exist in just a couple of days.

The thought of death had never really scared me before, but now it did. I didn't know how I was to be executed. Would it be fast? Would I pass quickly? Would it be painful or gruesome? Would there be multiple people as witnesses? Where would it happen? Would there be any mourning for me when I was gone? What would it be like to be dead? Would I be reincarnated? I had no idea what it would be like and that scared me.

As I was pondering these thoughts and questions in my head a guard called me over. I guess a whole day had already passed since hearing the sentence and it was time for my last meeting. "Your lucky day." the guard told me as he pushed me into a room.

"Mom!" I yelled with excitement. I ran towards her and noticed that she had been crying because her cheeks were a little red and moist. We hugged. It was the tightest hug I had ever felt. As we were hugging, I noticed that the walls all had windows with guards looking through them. We were being watched, but at least this time I wasn't talking to her through some intercom in the ceiling. I was still glad to see her.

"Mom." I said sternly, "I want you to know," but I didn't have time to finish before she cut me off. "I know." she said with a smile on her face. "You didn't kill him." She knew me better than to assume that I'd actually kill somebody. She knew that I would cause some trouble and get into fights, but I would never go all the way and take somebody's life. That just wasn't in me. She'd told me that she'd tried talking to the government, but to no avail. The evidence was all phony, she said, but they wanted it to stick on me because I was a dreamer. They would stop at nothing to try and justify executing me because of this. Dreamers never get off easy. We talked for 20 minutes which was so relieving and comforting. I needed it. It felt as if everything seemed fine and okay talking with my mom. I wasn't even thinking about the next day when I would be done away with. All worries seemed to just disappear for that short time that I was with her. We didn't talk much about what would happen tomorrow. Instead, we talked about good memories we'd had throughout our life. It was the most positive conversation I'd had in a long time.

After about 20 minutes a buzzer went off in our room and I knew we were done. The guard came in and I gave my mom a big hug. This huge fear wave came over me quickly and I didn't want to let go of my mom. The guard initially just told us to stop hugging, but after what seemed like a millisecond of not listening, he came over to pry me off my mother. "NO!" I yelled emotionally. Another guard came in, but they still had little success in separating us, when all of sudden I felt a big sting on my back. They started hitting me with their guard sticks which felt like getting hit with a thick branch with spikes on it. I still managed to hold onto my mother just until they hit her too. I let go immediately as she gasped from the pain of the blow. "STOPPPP." I yelled emphatically. They dragged me out with their sticks aimed at me as if warning me not to fight anymore.

I managed to see my mom mouth "Del." to me as I was leaving. My eyes were red and blurry from crying as I was thrown into my cell again. It was hard to see anything. Thankfully Del came to me and grabbed my arm and guided me towards my spot in the room.

After gathering myself and having my vision return to normal, I looked at Del as if expecting him to confirm something. There was nothing. He had a look on his face that was like, "Why you are looking at me like that?" I didn't understand, but I was still too emotionally drained to dig any further with him.

Two guards with sticks at their sides walked in front of our cell. I knew the time had come. I got nervous, but I was going to go without any resistance. My fighting days were done. "Skade." one of the guards said in a firm powerful voice as if he wasn't going to ask again. I got up from out of my spot in the back of the cell and started to walk towards them. He put his hand on my shoulder and motioned me out of the room. We were out of the room, but just before the door was closed one of my cell mates started shaking dramatically. I've seen a lot of crazy, like real crazy things in my life, but this was near the top of the list. His whole body started contorting in directions that I didn't think were possible. He was making grunting noises as if he was experiencing a lot of pain which I didn't doubt for a second. Some weird looking substance was coming out of his mouth, but I couldn't look long enough to figure out what it was. All my cell mates started yelling for help.

Del ran up to the guards, "Aren't you going to help?" Both guards almost in sync took their arms off me and half-heartedly yelled for more help down the hall. They rushed back into the room and put their hands on my cell mate as if that would calm him down. As soon as they put their hands on him though it was like he was totally fine. I was so confused. One moment his body was going crazy and the next he was completely still.

He looked directly at the two guards, but his look was one of treachery, which confused me even more. "Thanks" he said coldly and sarcastically. All the cell mates started beating down on the two guards. The two guards had no chance against my seven cell mates. They were all tough and cunning dudes too. It didn't take long for them to knock the guard's unconscious and then they all made their way out of the room while I was still standing there in awe.

"We're breaking out of here." said Voo as he passed by me.

"Come on," Del said as he grabbed me as he ran past me, "We're getting you out of here".

Thankfully for us we knew the way out of the cell house because we've navigated it every day on our way out to do community service. There were no cameras and it seemed as if the half- hearted call by the guards went unheard because there weren't any guards in the halls. "It must be really bad out there," said Del as we were running up to a T in the hall. I didn't entirely know what that meant, but I kept running. Del and I were in the back of the group and as we approached the split off at the hall, I started to go left but Del grabbed me and held me back.

"What are you doing?" I said sternly, knowing that left was the way out.

Del smirked, "We're going this way" he said, "and we don't have time to argue, trust me." Just them I remembered the sign that read "STAY CLOSE TO DEL." As my other cell mates continued to leave as if they had no idea we'd stopped. I reluctantly followed Del down the right hallway. "Change into a Lex guard," he told me. I did it without thinking, just before we passed another official strolling down the hall as if nothing out of the ordinary was happening. We were about 10 feet in front of him when he looked at us with a confused face.

"What are you doing with him?" The guard said cautiously.

I hesitated which probably didn't look that good, but just before I could answer Del blurted out, "I'm getting transferred," he said casually. I simply nodded my head. Guess that didn't fool him because he had no cuffs on but now that we were within feet of him Del lunged himself at him and knocked the guard down. The guard managed to get a yell out for help before Del knocked him out cold. I turned back to myself, and I didn't feel drained from shifting, probably because I was so energized from all the events that were happening right then. Del grabbed the card around the neck of the guard which was used to open the doors. We passed another cell room just like ours and Del opened the door. "Go that way!" He said as he pointed in the direction behind us. They didn't need to be told twice. They all got up and bolted in the direction Del was pointing.

Del and I continued down the cellhouse making left turns and right turns like he knew exactly where he was going. He didn't hesitate at any spot. He used the key card to open a couple doors. We'd been running through the halls for 2 minutes which made me realize how much bigger the cellhouse actually was. I guess we'd only been staying in the front part of the cell house so our distance to the outdoors was very short.

Every cell room we passed we opened the door and told them to run for it but to not follow us. "Almost-" Del took in a breath, "There". We came to a door which had a sign on top that said "JACOBY". We opened the room with the card. There were cabinets everywhere and each was full of folders with papers in them. He went straight to this cabinet and opened the third drawer down and grabbed two folders. I was still too out of breath from running, so I didn't have a chance to ask him what they were, but I saw a picture of me on one of the folders. Just as quickly as we entered the room, we left it. This whole time while we were running it hadn't occurred to me how there was only one guard that we passed throughout the whole cell house.

"Where were all the guards?" I thought to myself. We approached another seemingly ordinary door that I thought would lead us into some other never-ending hallway. As Del opened the door though I could immediately feel the heat from the outdoors.

I could also hear something strange. I didn't know what it was, but it sounded terrifying and big because I couldn't even hear myself think it was so loud. It was multiple high-pitched screeches as if a giant file was grinding down a mountain. Then I saw my mother. She was in a big black van in the driver's seat. She had a smile on her face which turned into astonishment as we approached the car. "Skade." I saw her mouth at me. We opened the door at the back of the van, and Del and I piled in. "It worked," she shouted because even inside the van the noise was still very apparent. It sounded like there was a little surprise in her mouth as if she didn't think it would actually work. I was still unsure about everything that was going on, but we didn't have time to chat because just as we hopped in the car chaos erupted from behind us and to our left. There was a big blue figure and lots of Lex guards and other citizens trying to avoid being trampled by the thing. "Del." my mother said, which surprised me because I had never told her about Del.

"On it" he yelled back as if he knew what my mother was talking about. Just then he held out his hands in front of him and then they started to glow. If you've ever felt time stop then you know what I'm talking about, but if not, I have no idea how to explain it. Everyone around us, even the big creature, seemed to stop and we kept going. I have heard of Krimps power, but I had no idea how they did it exactly. I was in complete awe.

It only lasted long enough for us to get around a little group of people in front of us and then Del breathed in deeply and when he exhaled it was as if everyone returned to normal like nothing had happened. "Thanks!" my mom yelled from up front. Del looked like he was going to pass out, so I didn't ask him how he did that, but I just helped him put his head against a pillow that was in the back. I noticed the pillow was from my apartment. My mom must have brought it. Del rested his head against the pillow, and it looked like he was going to fall asleep. As I looked at him, I suddenly realized I was tired from shifting and it was finally kicking in after all the adrenaline and energy had now passed me. My mom instinctively threw back another pillow and I rested my head on it.

"Thanks." I said without yelling, now that the sound from the monster wasn't as loud. "20 minutes." my mom said back. I didn't know what that meant, but I was out before I could ask.

In what seemed like a snap of the finger I was awake in the back of the van. I don't think I slept very well because I was still very tired, and I vaguely remember moving a lot from side to side which

I assumed was because my mom was swerving in and out of crowds and traffic on our way. I peeked outside the window and saw some big mountain peaks which I'd only heard of before. We were in the far North end of the city close to the mountain range.

"Is he here?" said a familiar voice as my mom opened the back of the van.

"Macrill!" I said energetically as if I was no longer tired. I got out of the van and saw Macrill standing there with the biggest smile on his face. We embraced.

"I thought I'd never see you again" he said.

"You won't believe-" I said as I was suddenly cut off by Del.

"We don't have much time." he said concerningly, "They're going to leave soon."

"What? Who?" I blurted out.

Then my mother chimed in, "Yes, we have to hurry."

"What's going on?" I said with a confused look on my face.

Then with a serious face my mother said, "We're going to meet the Dreamers."

The Clud Attack

Unless you really like hiking through hills in extremely hot conditions with little rest and sustenance then I wouldn't recommend going through the Eyup mountains. Even with all the dense brush and trees, there was still not enough shade to cool us down with the two stars shining down on us constantly. Most of the bushes had thorns and sharp leaves which easily scratch any exposed skin upon contact. The trees were all green around the base with bright purple divots going all the way to the top. They were very smooth and had a clean textured look. The trunks ranged in size from a foot in diameter to six feet. They were sturdy and very big looking. The tree bases were a stark contrast to the ground which was a very crumbly light brown dirt. There wasn't too much grass on Ooba compared to Zazri and other planets because of the extreme heat and sunlight.

We were all tired from a chaotic day, but we were hastily trekking through the trees and bushes. We didn't have time to rest. The little provisions we did have would only be enough to hold us over for a couple of days. We had various assortments of fruit and breads, but my mother didn't pack anything more, fearing that it would slow us down too much. We had little reserves of water hoping that we could find some in the mountains. We hiked along one river for a couple of hours which trickled down the mountain. It carved a path through rocks, mud, tree roots and everything that kept it from making it to the bottom of the mountain. I wondered how there could be so much water because it rarely rained on

Jacoby and I didn't think the weather on Ooba was much different than Jacoby, but here there were rivers, I guess. The river didn't look clean enough to drink. "There will be others" my mother said half-heartedly as we walked by it. It didn't sound like she was convinced herself that there would be others.

It was weird seeing clouds here because it seemed so foreign. Last time I remember seeing clouds was on Zazri. I've heard of some rumors about these mountains, but I never figured they'd actually be true. We saw some interesting looking skinny cows that were bright red, and they had 6 feet. I couldn't tell how tall they were exactly from seeing them at a distance, but they looked well over 6 feet. It's said that they aren't shy of eating flesh. Hopefully we wouldn't get to know them well enough to find out.

We were heading along what seemed to be a path that was used frequently. All the dirt had divots in it making it appear that people had walked through there before. The trail would go dirt to grass and bushes all around and back just as quickly. Luckily for us it also crossed other small streams occasionally which were cleaner than the first river we saw. We would drink up the water like it was the last time we were going to see water again. We would dip ourselves in to cool us down which was a life saver. Macrill started getting some blisters on his neck due to the exposure of the suns and it was draining him rapidly. Our breaks became more frequent and longer as our journey progressed. We knew we had to keep going so we wouldn't get left behind, but after every stop it got harder and harder to keep pressing forward. The mountain became steeper. The brush seemed to lighten up which was nice, but it also meant less shade of the little amount that we did have. The clouds that were up around the mountains were not thick enough to provide sufficient coverage from the stars. Every once in a while, we would pass what seemed to be the remains of a little camp. There was a bigger area that was flattened down, or as flat as you could get a campsite on a mountainside. There would be rocks in a circle with some black ash inside. There were scraps of meat hanging in the trees, which was common in the mountains according to the stories. I guess they were offered to the creatures in the mountains so they wouldn't harm the people on the mountain.

"We're getting close," my mother said, using all her breath. It was no easy trek through the mountains, and it drained all of us. I didn't know how she was so sure, to me it seemed like we were barely halfway up the mountain.

"It would take us another couple of hours to get to the top," I thought. And as far as I remember I didn't see any sign that said YOU'RE ALMOST THERE, or JUST A LITTLE FURTHER. We didn't pass any of that.

We staggered up to a small little valley with a pond. "Now I could get used to this." Macrill said after catching his breath. The view was stunning. One sun was going down just below the mountain and when we turned around the other sun was coming up above the mountain ridge line. Even with the little cloud cover above us it was still clear enough to see very pretty colors being reflected from the atmosphere. Light green with a warm purple in the sky contrasted the dark blue lake and dark green trees. We were all stunned by the beauty of the scenery. We could hear some animals making noises in the brush which made it even more peaceful. At that moment I felt like my memory of whatever was going on in my life didn't mean anything.

How quickly it changed. What seemed like moments after taking in the little that Ooba had to offer, we were being held at knife point. Macrill, Del, my mother and I were all at the mercy of a knife at our throats. These were the Mountain Men. It was said that they were part nature, part human. Their faces were covered, which I was happy about because the rest of their body was some sight. One arm was made of wood with very sharp thorns coming out of what would be their fingers. The other arm was constantly shifting to blend in with the background. No matter what angle you were looking at it, it would almost look invisible. You could only catch the silhouette of it right as you looked at it from a different per-spective, then it would quickly blend in with the new angle. The bottom half of their body looked like a moose. They were roughly 8 feet tall. I've been in quite a few fights in my life, but this was not a fight we could win. They bound our hands. Then they took us to their camp. After seeing the Mountain Men and their camp I wish they would have just ended our lives. I think it could have been better. At their camp the Mountain Men no longer had their faces covered. "Whoa." I thought. They had a bear looking head with 2 big brown eyes and two smaller brown eyes above the bigger eyes and closer together. They had small round white horns. They also had little wings for ears coming out of the side of their heads.

They put us in a little hut and locked the door. I'd be lying to myself if I said it was hotter outside than inside. This was a hot feeling that I had never experienced before. All the buildings on Ooba had a cooling system and reflector shields to keep the heat out. This little hut didn't have either. Just imagine being put in a little box just big enough to keep you in it and it was on the verge of catching fire, then times that by 10 and that's what it felt like in this little box. Honestly, I don't know how there weren't more fires on Ooba but somehow the Jubi creators of Ooba made everything fire resistant. The only plus side of being inside was not having to look at the Mountain Men. If we looked at them long enough, they'd probably just eat us. There was also a big water bowl connected to the hut in the corner of the room. We were exhausted as it was, but being in this hut made it even worse and we drank about half the water in the first 2 minutes of being in the hut.

"There goes our chances." my mother said sadly with her head hanging down. I still didn't quite understand what everyone was meaning about our little "escape the city and find the dreamers" mission. Like who are the dreamers? Why would we seek refuge from them? What would they be able to offer us? It seemed as if every time I tried to ask about it, we were interrupted, or they just pushed my questions aside.

"Well," Macrill said, "Now what do we do?" Del took in a deep sigh and shrugged. My mother just sighed.

"For starters," I chimed in, "We know we got to get out of here. Question is, how?" It seemed quiet outside for most of the day, but we knew there was a Mountain Man on guard all day that would bring us small rations of food and enough water to refill our bowl in the corner. It was never dark enough to try and escape by night. They were all bigger than us so it would be difficult to fight our way out. They also knew the territory way better than we did so even if somehow, we did manage to escape it wouldn't take them long to track us down again. And if they decided to let us go, we wouldn't make it far anyway because we were all so weak due to the lack of food and water that we had. On top of that my mother started to get sick, which was no surprise to me considering the circumstances. I was more surprised that nobody else was sick, including myself. Just about anybody would feel sick after being in this hut for a couple of hours and it seemed like we were here for a couple of days. And believe it or not we were more than happy to be outside even without our protective gear than being stuck in this little shack. Whenever the guards came into our hut to fill our water and give us our food it felt like a cool breeze coming in from outside. It didn't last long, but we relished it whenever it happened. The breeze felt like ice on our skin which was very relieving from the heat inside the hut.

We discussed a couple of different plans to break out. We came up with a couple, but none of them seemed like they would work. We were very doubtful about the whole thing, and it didn't seem realistic or attainable. We tried to get information out of the guards whenever they were around to fill our water and give us food. It was always to no avail because they never responded. Usually, they would just tell us to be quiet and would push us if we got in their way at all. We weren't getting anything out of the guards.

We all knew we had to do something because we wouldn't last much longer in that hut and we had no idea what the Mountain Men wanted to do to us, but it couldn't be good considering how they treated us. We decided on a plan and were going to go through with it as soon as the guards came in and opened our door. We had thought that we could all take down the guard somewhat quickly and quietly without calling any attention from the others. Thankfully our hut was a little bit off from their little village. We would lock him in the hut and run in the opposite direction of the village. That was our extremely elaborate plan. Pathetic I know but trust me our other plans were worse.

We were all getting ready when the time came. I was in charge of taking out his feet as soon as he was done filling our water. Del would gag his mouth, which would have been terrifying because their teeth were so big, and their mouth was ginormous. My mother and Macrill would both tackle him and tie down his arms. Del would only be able to slow down time for a brief second for us because if he used any more then he wouldn't be able to run for very long.

We could hear our guard approaching so we knew it was time. Now or never, we thought. We heard him right outside our door. He was fidgeting with the keys. I was standing right next to the water bowl looking at the door. He opened it, but this time I saw beyond the Mountain Man standing at the door. There was another who was further away as if he was waiting for him, but he wasn't paying much attention to us. He was kicking his feet through the grass and looking at something on his arm. I tensed and I knew Del saw it too because he was right next to me. We looked at each other and at my mother and Macrill who both managed to understand something was wrong by the looks on our faces. My mother nodded at both of us as if we were still going to go through with it.

The Mountain Man put our food next to the door and was headed towards the water bowl with a big canteen full of water. Did I mention that Mountain Men were big? I mean he was huge. He seemed even bigger now than before, but this was probably because I now had to summon the courage to take him down and that was daunting. I was not ready, but as soon as he stopped pouring out of his canteen I sprang for his feet. Del immediately went to close his mouth with both hands. As soon as I put my arms around his legs I was forced backwards and his whole body came down on me. Macrill and my mother had done a good job at taking him down. I just wish I was on the other side of his body instead of underneath him. I was worried that the other mountain guard was sure to have seen or heard something, but I didn't hear anyone yelling from outside our hut. Del, somehow beyond my knowledge, managed to shut his mouth. It took all my strength and willpower to keep him from breaking free. I could tell Macrill, and my mom were struggling to keep him down. I figured in about 5 seconds he would break free. Then he stopped squirming. I managed to get out from under him and I was trying to catch my breath when I saw my mom holding the water canteen in her hand above the Mountain Man. She hit him. Del slowed down time for just a second so my mom could let go and hit him over the head. We were all stunned. What added more to our astonishment was right after that, my mom called over the other guard. "What are you doing?" I asked my mother, confused.

Before she could answer she yelled out at the other guard, "Hey, he just passed out. Come and help him up." Then she turned to-wards me and mumbled "Here we go again."

I thought, "this can't be good." As soon as he walked in, Del froze time again and we hit him over the head with the canteen. Del didn't need to stop time for too long for us to do this, but I could tell it still took quite a bit out of him because as we were running away, I had to help him stay balanced as we ran.

We didn't look back. We probably only made it 200 yards when we heard a bunch of roars and yells from the Mountain Men. We knew the guards would be okay because there was no way they would die from one hit from a single water canteen.

We knew they would be after us, so we ran even faster than before.

Running through the brush and small creeks was no easy task. There were weird creatures that we had to avoid. And rocks we had to be careful not to trip over. We even had to swim through this deep river at one point. We could hear the Mountain Men gaining on us because their sounds gradually began getting louder and louder. This wasn't all that surprising to me because they did have 4 legs, so I just assumed they'd be faster than us. As soon as I reached the other side of the river I turned around and saw them on the far side of the river. They'd gained on us so fast. I knew we wouldn't make it much further especially since Del still wasn't at full strength. We made it up the next little hill and they were already out of the water. I can't think of any scarier sight than seeing about twenty-five full grown Mountain Men chasing you down like their lives depended on it. Most of them were without weapons because they probably didn't need any, but some still had guns that they fired in our direction. Luckily for us even with their 4 eyes they couldn't aim very good. They were 40 feet from us when suddenly we saw a dirt crawler which is a type of vehicle here on Ooba that was headed straight for us. "They've come." my mom yelled with hope in her voice. It was going to be close I thought. And I had no idea who "they" were, but anybody was better than the Mountain Men. The crawler swerved into a complete stop right in front of us and the doors popped open. We all jumped in, and the driver, whose face I couldn't recognize, peeled out. Two Mountain Men managed to get a grip on the crawler, but the driver made quick work of them, and their ride came to a quick and bumpy end. I didn't know who was driving, but I had a feeling I knew him though I wasn't sure how.

We didn't seem to slow down in the slightest. He kept his foot on the pedal the whole time. So, I found out that he was part of the dreaming society. I had no idea what that was, though my mother had tried to talk to me about it before. Apparently, he didn't like his real name, and everybody just called him Truue for some reason. He was also from Zazri and had escaped during the time the Clud invaded. There was something strange about him though that didn't seem to fit right. I didn't know what it was about him, but something seemed off. My mom knew him somehow, but I had no idea how or why. We didn't talk a whole lot because we were all so exhausted after what we'd been through the past week. Thankfully he had some water and food in the crawler, so we had something to fill ourselves with.

We were going pretty fast through the mountains, passing all types of terrain that I had no idea existed on Ooba. There was snow, lava, little jungles full of slime looking stuff where water normally would be. They were like slime rivers. We passed through an area that seemed to have fire all around us and it was totally normal. The dirt crawler didn't have any trouble with any of the terrains. The scenery seemed to change every five minutes as we sped through hills, mountains, and big plateaus. There were weird creatures that we would pass every once in a while. These creatures would probably scare away the Mountain Men they were so creepy and funky looking. I was glad we only saw them at a distance and not up close. Some of them we only got a glimpse of because we were passing through so fast.

Suddenly we started to slow down drastically. I didn't think anything of it until I saw a look of concern on the driver. "BRACE YOURSELF" he shouted. Before I could grab hold of anything to brace myself on, our entire crawler got rocked and we went tumbling into the air. It all happened so fast that I don't remember the details. I remember still being conscious when our crawler finally stopped rolling. We were upside down and somehow; I only had a few cuts on my face and arms. My back was pretty sore, but I still could move. "We have to get out" Truue said. I didn't argue with him. He knew better than I did. I could hear something about 200 hundred yards away that sounded like a giant flame thrower. This is not good. Del was beat up pretty bad, so Macrill and I had to help him get out of the crawler. My mother got out fine as did Truue. "Start digging" Truue ordered. We all used whatever we could to help us shovel the dirt. I just used my hands. Macrill found a stick to help him while Del also used his only good hand. Thankfully, the dirt terrain we were in was extremely soft, so we made good progress. The sound kept getting louder and louder as we continued digging. I had no idea why we were digging, but I knew we would not be able to outrun the thing considering what it did to our crawler. We only dug about a foot deep, just long enough for our bodies to lay in them. The sound only sounded like it was 50 yards away from us and I could feel the heat, I was too nervous to look, but it had to be extremely terrifying whatever it was. I feared going into shock if I saw it, so I just kept my head down. "Get in" Truue said as he laid in and started covering himself with the dirt. We all followed suit though I was very doubtful because the creature was so close now that he could probably easily see us. After covering our bodies, we took a deep breath and covered our heads with dirt. Our bodies were completely covered just as an extreme source of heat came over us. We could feel it right above us and it had stopped as it got over us. The creature seemed confused as it moved back and forth right over us like it was trying to process where we were. I didn't know how much longer I could hold my breath. I could start to feel myself blacking out from lack of oxygen.

If you enjoy being choked or drowning then I would highly recommend trying this, but otherwise I would stay as far away from it as possible.

Next thing I remember I was in a little hut. I was alone and the heat was killing me. There was a little bucket in the corner and then it hit me. I recognized this hut as the hut we just got out of from the Mountain Men. I heard giant footsteps coming. They opened the door and there were two huge Mountain Men standing there with huge grins on their faces. It seemed as if they were telling me that something way worse than them was waiting for me. They took me to their village. There were lines of people gathering on both sides of our path staring at me. I was terrified. Most of them were growling at me as I passed. We headed up to what I guessed was their village's only tourist attraction. It was a big open structure. There was a very majestic, pointed dome. It overhung on the front end and only had 3 big pillars on the back end. There were beautiful flowers that I've never seen before. They were wrapped around the pillars as well. The stairs leading up to the structure were very wide and multiple feet between each step. There was a big open mat in the middle of the ground with a couple of benches around the outside. There were some Mountain Men sitting on them which looked kind of interesting because they had 4 legs, so it just looked weird. They also looked older than most of the other Mountain Men. They pushed me into the middle and had me stand there. All the towns' people had followed us and were standing around the structure looking at me. There was one other chair that was empty at the back of the structure. I started to hear a large sound climbing up the mountain. It sounded like giant propellers. Nobody said anything, but as the noise got louder, eyes started to turn towards where the noise was coming from.

It was a big black flyer. I've seen these types of flyers before, but this one was different and much bigger. These were the most common flying vehicles here on Ooba, but you didn't see too many of them in Jacoby. They were mainly found in other parts of Ooba. It looked like a giant sideways diamond. It had two big wings coming off either side straight up into the air. I had no idea where the ship was going to land because there wasn't exactly a landing pad anywhere nearby. I guess they knew that because it just hovered over the ground on the edge of the village and a giant door opened and a ramp came out, so it was touching the ground. There were 5 of them that came out. There were two Jubis, a Krimp, a Gri and a Lex who I knew. It was Dakool. Dakool didn't seem to be in charge though because as they got off the ramp, they all made way for a Jubi who came down last. I had no idea who he was, but he seemed to be a powerful man. He's the one who sat down on the chair under the structure. He was a very large man. He made the Mountain Men look small. He had a gun strapped to his leg that had a small dagger sticking out of the end of it. He had a big bald spot on the left side of his head right above his ear. He had a big staff in his left hand which was pure black, and it had a red stripe down both sides of it. The top part of the staff looked like roots with little parts of the staff going in all directions. It looked like the same material as all the Clud ships. Same color and it had the same aura as if it came from some dark place in the universe. That about sums up the Clud, but why would he have a staff that looked like it belonged to or came from the Clud.? Who was this dude? What did he want with me?

He hit his staff on the ground as if to call for everyone's attention, but everyone was already looking at him and nobody was talking. You could barely even hear noises from other creatures around their little village. "Skade." he said. His voice was very deep and raspy as if two stones were being scraped against each other. It sent a chill throughout my entire body. What scared me more, however, was the fact that he knew my name. I had clearly not known this dude. It would have been plausible for Dakool to tell him my name, but I had a feeling he knew me and not just my name. Before he could get anything else out, I sprang to life.

I was hoisted out of the dirt. Truue was grabbing my arm and noticed that something was wrong. "You good?" he asked. "Uhh yeah," I said, "totally fine." For some reason I didn't tell him what I saw, which was okay because we had other things to worry about. Before I could catch my breath after being buried alive, we quickly got Del, Macrill, and my mother out.

"We have got to keep moving." Truue said as his eyes kept streaking back and forth as if he were speaking it into existence, "They'll be back." I still had no idea what was chasing us, but I didn't have time to ask. I just knew that the creature thing or whatever it was, was extremely hot and very big.

We made good headway for the next 20 minutes towards the city of Bagger. We could see it as we made our way up to a hill. The city looked so different compared to Jacoby. I couldn't see it very well because it was still a way out, but it still seemed very different from the little we could see. We made our way down the hill and the city went out of view. We felt a hope that we hadn't felt since leaving Jacoby. Everything seemed to be going wrong since we left Jacoby, but seeing the city inspired us to keep moving forward. As we neared the bottom of the hill we were surrounded by thick bushes and trees all around with the sand at our feet. There was a loud grumbling noise in the distance, and we knew what it was. Without saying anything we all started to run while trying to stay quiet somehow. We knew the fiery creature was close to us before and it was still roaming around. We were unlucky to cross its path in the first place considering how big the mountain range was in which it roamed. Of course, it was our luck to run into it twice in the same day. Running through the sand was hard and it drained the little energy that we had very quickly. The trees and bushes finally cleared up and we could see Bagger. We heard the sound behind us getting louder and louder. There was about 200 yards from the edge of the forest where we were to the city. There were no trees ahead of us and the sand appeared to die off about 40 yards in. There were small rocks and boulders just after the sand ended, all the way to the city. If we crossed the sand, we would lose our ability to hide from the creature, but we may make it to the city before the creature reached us. "We could just wait it out." I mentioned. Which I regretted saying as soon as it came out of my mouth. Everyone was tired as it was, and we needed fresh water and cooling in the buildings that Bagger would offer. We bolted for it. We came to the end of the sand, but we didn't stop to re-evaluate our situation. Everyone just kept on going. I did a quick head turn and could see above the trees a large form emitting a lot of heat. The creature was very dark black on the inside with red and orange around him. For all I know its body was comprised of fire and more fire. I quickly turned and followed suit behind my companions. We slowly made our way over small boulders and un-steady rocks. About halfway to the city from the forest we knew we wouldn't be able to make it. We could feel the heat coming in fast behind us. The heat was almost unbearable. Even if we had a good protective suit we would have been burnt very quickly. There was no coverage with the rocks.

I don't know how, but I could hear another noise faintly coming from the city in our direction. Which must have been very loud when there was no fiery creature around to drown out its noise. Looking at the creature was hard, and it burnt the eyes, yet I no-ticed it had stopped just as it got past the sand. I wondered why it had stopped and thought maybe it needed to be over the sand for some reason, but I was thankful it had stopped. We were about 20 yards away from the creature and we could feel its extreme heat. The noise from the city began to get exponentially louder when suddenly, the creature was hit with a giant bomb of black dust. The creature staggered backwards and bellowed so loud the ground be-neath us felt like it was going to part in two. Nobody in their right mind would have assumed the monster was content and happy because it was clear it wanted to get us. Just before the creature could gather its strength to come in our direction again it was hit by another bomb of black dust which sent it back again. I heard the noise directly over us now. It was a small, squared ship about

40 feet above us with the letters CK under it. I had no idea what CK meant but in the moment it didn't matter. The ships' engines were extremely loud. It had one large cannon sticking out of the front which was firing big black rocks. As I was looking, it had fired another rock directly at the creature. As the rock exploded off the creature some small pieces flew in our direction. It felt smooth, but it irritated the skin. As I was holding a piece of the debris, I looked down and realized what it was. I hadn't noticed it before because I was wearing shoes, but the rocks that were coming out of the cannon on the ship were the same type of rocks we were walking on. I've heard about this type of rock before. On the planets where this rock was accessible it was used to fight off the Clud. Its contents were highly acidic to a lot of races and creatures. We didn't have any on Zazri so fighting the Clud off was harder than it was for other planets. I guess it made sense why the Clud had not yet attacked Ooba as they could probably sense the rock.

Thankfully after another couple of rocks were shot at the fiery creature it turned and headed back towards the forest and mountains. Just as the creature turned and left so did the ship. I thought maybe they would have picked us up or dropped us off some supplies or something, but we didn't get any special treatment other than them saving our lives. I don't know how long the creature could have withstood being on the rocks, but I figured it would have slowed it down, just not enough before it got to us.

Entering the city like a bunch of homeless people was exactly what the people around us saw. Bagger was much bigger than Jacoby. There were way more people. The buildings seemed more advanced. The black rocks surrounded the entire city. There were more ships flying above us. There seemed to be more vehicles in the streets as well. There were giant screens on a lot of the buildings. One showed news from another planet being invaded by Clud. The planet was full of strange races that I had never seen before. Some had gotten away and managed to capture what was happening to their planet as they fled. Another screen showed this group of Jubi with the caption "The Builders Best" and all of them were holding some tool in their hands. Another screen just showed a clip of the creature that had been chasing us being hit with giant rocks from a CK ship. The footage was coming from a building at the edge of the city, and it was mainly focused above us, so we weren't in the video. Another video board showed some buildings that looked familiar that were burning. I recognized the building and its surroundings. It was the building for all the workers that kept intact the habitats and ecosystems on the outside of Jacoby. "Unrest in Jacoby Continues" the video read. It had been a couple of days since we left Jacoby and it seemed to be in a worse state than ever. It just showed the workers' building in flames, but I'm certain the rest of the city was probably just as bad or worse. "That's not good." I said stating the obvious.

"No." my mother said. Taking in a deep sigh, "It's not good at all."

Thankfully we didn't see any videos or signs about us. You would think that after "committing murder" and breaking out of the jail house the government would be after you. They must have some pretty bad stuff going for them not to be worried about us. I wasn't complaining about it.

Here in the city of Bagger there wasn't nearly as much chaos as there was in Jacoby, but it seemed they had their fair share of troubles as well. There were dozens of ships coming in from the big shuttle just above Ooba. People from other planets who came to Ooba had to pass by a giant shuttle ship surrounding Ooba. There were lots of security measures in place to prevent unwanted races or creatures getting into Ooba. The Clud were clearly continuing their destructive paths to rid the universe of all living species except for the Clud. The races that were exiting the ships coming in were not familiar to me. They had white rubber looking skin. They had three triangular eyes. None of them had hair. They looked like humans in the sense that they had two arms and two legs. They had a tail coming out from their back side. They had another smaller looking tail coming out of each elbow. They were all the same height too and were very muscular.

There were some other ships coming in that carried some more Lexlands. The city of Bagger was one of the bigger cities that took in refugees of other planets. When I first arrived on Ooba we passed through here, but it was a long time ago and I didn't remember much. I remember being cleared by the big shuttles orbiting Ooba. Every ship that enters and exits Ooba needs to be cleared. Getting clearance is no easy process. Essentially, to leave you need the permission of the creators of Ooba. I knew the Jubi had created Ooba and finished it just before the attacks of the Clud on planets in the universe. I didn't know exactly who of all the Jubi had created it. They were rarely talked about, and you never heard of them. I didn't even know if they were still alive. To get into Ooba you just needed to pass a test given by the security of Ooba that states that you're fleeing from the Clud. Ooba was created for the Jubi initially, but as the Clud began their attacks they allowed refugees to stay on Ooba only if they were fleeing from the Clud.

The Clud began their attacks on different planets around 9 years ago. They attacked Zazri a year after their initial attack. Because the Clud need meat or flesh to survive they began invading other planets. The Clud came from the planet Cludula. Cludula was right next to Zazri which was usually between them and the nearest star. They didn't get much sun, which was a perfect environment for them to turn into the creatures they are now after all the ash from the eruption of the volcano covered their planet. Before they changed, they were normal creatures, but that ash did something to their chemical and physical makeup causing them to become who they are now. They weren't the friendliest before, but after they turned, they were anything but friendly. Now they were attacking all creatures they could to survive.

Thankfully there were no Clud on this planet. Due to the two close stars around Ooba, and the Black Flower can't grow here. This is the safest planet in the universe, very sunny and lots of security measures in place to protect against the Clud.

After wandering through the streets to find somewhere we could get some food and water and be inside, we found a bigger building that seemed to have all of it. We entered the building and we felt so relieved. The cool air against our skin felt like a cold current running along the skin. The building was so different than any building in Jacoby. Here in Bagger, it seemed that the buildings were opposites of Jacoby. The upper third were the houses of all the people and the bottom two thirds were their working areas. This building was advertised outside as a "whatever you need" like building. We saw stores of all sorts manned by all types of creatures. After living in Jacoby and only seeing Jubi, Lexlands, Krimps, and Gri, I had forgotten how there were in fact other races here on Ooba. It seemed that this building was one of the busiest in Bagger because it was so crowded. We felt like a shipment of merchandise just being tossed and pushed with the flow of the people. In the very middle was a moving platform that rotated quicker than expected. If I wasn't being held up on all sides by the people around me, I would have toppled over as soon as my foot stepped onto the moving platform. The platform spun clockwise and standing on it for too long would make one want to vomit. We got pushed off the platform right in front of an all-meat shop. They had all types of meat from all types of creatures. Thankfully things were cheap here and we still had some money that my mom had brought with her.

The "Fire Burger" was good, but so hot. I had to drink a couple glasses of this special drink the store offered to help with the heat. I didn't ask where the meat came from because I didn't want to confirm my suspicions after encountering a flaming creature earlier that day. My mother got some weird looking sandwich as did Macrill. Del got a different burger that was bigger than his head. The thing was ginormous, but he managed to eat it all. I wondered what people around us thought about us as we ate our food. We ate it so fast, and we didn't leave any leftovers. We were messy too, considering all the crumbs around us and seeing how dirty our fingers were. Nobody seemed to make too big a deal about it though because everyone just seemed to go on their way. After finishing our food, we headed over to a store selling protective gear. We passed a couple of other stores selling random things, which gave me the impression that you really could find anything you needed in this building.

"And there are 7 more levels of stores." I thought to myself. Thankfully we had just enough to get some new protective gear for all of us. This protective gear was way more advanced and better than what was offered back in Jacoby. They were supposed to last for a total of 3 days before needing to regenerate. They fit very nicely and comfortably. We felt like completely new beings after getting this new gear and having a full stomach and a chance to just chill for a bit without worrying about something or somebody coming after us. That feeling didn't last long though. We found a bench to sit on that somehow wasn't being used by anyone in the building and were just resting amidst all the commotion and people around us.

"Are you Skade?" said an unfamiliar voice behind us. We turned around and saw a regular looking Jubi and a Krimp standing there. "Uh" I said confused, "Skade?"

"The one who killed my brother." The Jubi spoke up firmly with a disappointed look on his face as if he knew I was playing dumb. We had just made it to what would be our new home. And had just eaten some good food and got new gear. We were resting from our long travels, and we just couldn't seem to catch a break. We were in Bagger for a grand total of 3 hours and somehow trouble had found us already. So many thoughts were flowing through my head, and everyone kept quiet until I heard somebody in the crowd yell "RUN." I had no idea who yelled it, but it didn't matter as soon as we heard it Macrill, Del, Truue, my mother, and I took off.

I'm Rescued by a Run-Away

Running away with a bloated stomach and little rest over a couple day span should not be on anybody's To-Do list. Sure, you feel a little energy rush, some adrenaline kicks in for a moment here and there, but it doesn't last long. The excitement that you think you would feel in a situation like this fades quickly. The most upsetting thing about being chased though was knowing that I shouldn't have been the one being chased in the first place. Somehow, I had been accused of murdering somebody who I didn't even know. I had no motive to kill anybody. I wouldn't profit anything and even if I had a motive, I don't think I could manage the task of taking somebody's life. I would argue that most people wouldn't wish pain on another individual let alone the death of somebody.

I guess the brother of the victim and I weren't on the same page. We barely made it around a corner when we heard a gunshot right behind us. We continued running, knowing that slowing down would mean the gunshot would be that much closer to hitting us. We were glad he wasn't the best aim, and he wasn't the fastest. His Krimp friend couldn't slow time down either because Del was with us. You see a Krimps ability to slow down time only works if all the Krimps around let it happen. We kept running past a couple side stores and lots of people. Nobody seemed to be worried about a mad man chasing a couple people with a gun and firing aimlessly in our direction. Nobody even tried to stop us or the people following us. But we couldn't run forever. Our bodies were still tired from our long journey through the mountains and our crazy encounters with the Mountain Men and some terrifying creatures.

My mom entered the building first. If I had to pick the building to run into for cover, I would not have chosen this one. Yeah, the building provided good cover to hide from the crazies chasing us, but we wouldn't last long ourselves in the building. The building only had one floor above ground, so from the outside it looked like a very small building compared to all the buildings surrounding it. As soon as we got inside, we felt instant humidity and heat. It was hotter inside the building than outside, which was very rare. "Where are we?" Macrill asked in amazement.

"I think I have an idea." Del said with a surprised look on his face, which would have been impossible to see through the smoke had I not been standing right next to him. "It's a mining building."

The room was very smoky, and all the walls were coated in black ash. There were a bunch of big holes with a sheet of metal mesh covering them that allowed black smoke to come out from down below and prevented people from falling into them. There were dim lights coming from under the holes as well. There was a big contraption in the middle of the room that was lit up in bright neon blue. It had to be very bright otherwise nobody would be able to find it. It was hard to guess just how big exactly the room was because we couldn't see very far through the smoke. We made our way towards the contraption which turned out to be the elevator.

It seemed the further down we went the harder it was to breathe and see. The buttons on the shaft went from 1 all the way to negative 12. I couldn't believe that there were so many levels underground, but we figured there'd be no way for the goons chasing us to find us in here. We got off on level 3. Thankfully we decided we wouldn't need to go down any further than the third level. We found some emergency head and body cases that were made for the miners to breathe normally without inhaling a bunch of unhealthy toxins from their labors. It was also partly made up of the same material as our new protective suits to help withstand the extreme heat.

There was a map right next to the elevator shaft that was also lit up in neon blue. Based on the map it seemed like the mine extended to a great distance to our left and our right. It looked like a big narrow tunnel. The ceiling was only 8 feet high. Del had to crouch down a little to avoid hitting his head. I don't how it could have run on for long without interfering with the foundations of the surrounding buildings. I figured we were too deep, but then I didn't know why it didn't run for a long time in all directions. Anyway, we found a small room which appeared to be a break room which had a handful of people in it. Somehow the break room wasn't as smoky or as hot due to some turbines they had in the room. I'm guessing by the expression on some of the workers faces that they didn't get many visitors down there because they knew as soon as we walked in the room that we didn't belong there. Still, we tried to look like we knew what we were doing, and we were part of the big mining family. The workers were all very muscular and had huge hands. Most of them were Jubis, but there was a fair share of other races in the room as well.

We sat down at a table that had some other workers on the other end. It seemed like they were on their break, and they were talking about stones or jewels it sounded like. One of the bigger workers in the room who was sitting at a different table got up and headed towards us. "Uh Oh" I said wearily, "this can't be good."

"You guys look like you could use a drink." He said to my surprise.

"Ummm" I managed to bleat out, still stunned at what he said. His hands had scratches and bruises all over them as if he'd just got in a fight, but his face was very warm and welcoming.

"Yeah we'd love one." I replied. "It's been a long day." Del and Macrill both nodded in unison like they were agreeing with me. He went back to his table, grabbed his big mug, and brought it over along with 4 cups. He poured out this thick blue ooze looking drink. I was hesitant to drink it, but Del apparently knew what it was because his face lit up as soon as he realized what it was. He downed his as soon as the stranger finished pouring his cup. I was still a little reluctant to try it. I put my lips to it and had a sip. It was hard to put down after the first taste, it was so good. Imagine the best blue raspberry you've ever had, mix it up with some very sweet sugar and a hint of mango flavoring and times that by 10 because that's what it tasted like. The aftertaste was the same as the original. It seemed to last very briefly in the throat, however. "Wow." I said shocked at what I had just drunk. "What was that?". Before he had a chance to respond, I felt very dizzy and started to lose my eyesight. Next thing I knew I was falling off my chair on the table and hit the ground knocked out cold.

"Whoa." I thought to myself. It's easy to tell when I'm dreaming because my life is crazy and wild often, so I knew I was in a dream. Sometimes dreams just come and that's the nature of them. You don't always know if you will dream, but we've learned from our culture and especially from my family that there are always a lot of meanings behind dreams. Sometimes they can help us visualize our emotions of what we're feeling in real life, but in different situations and circumstances. They often have implications for how we should act or what decisions we should make. They can even reveal our futures or the futures of others if we're given the chance to interpret others' dreams. Here on Ooba, we didn't get much opportunity to dream let alone interpret others dreams just because of the laws in place here. Our dreams almost always have double meanings, and it takes lots of experience and wisdom to know how to determine the meanings behind dreams.

I was sitting in a big open field full of white flowers. There was a slight breeze. It was 30 minutes before sunset. The temperature felt like a warmer spring back on Zazri. I laid down in the flowers, but I couldn't seem to stay still. I sat up and saw a little village up on a hill that seemed abandoned from a distance. I headed towards the village and quickly discovered that it was anything but abandoned. There were white rubber people that I had seen in Bagger all over the village. The village seemed to be in turbulence because the white rubber people were running and hiding in and behind anything that would cover them. Most of them had small guns that shot out a thick dark blue like laser. I saw a couple people who appeared to be injured but not enough to keep them from the fight. They would limp or have blood dripping off their clothes, but they were still fighting. As I got closer, I saw they were fighting a group of Jubi which I found very interesting. The planet I was on didn't exactly look like Ooba and I didn't think that the Jubi would live on a planet where the white rubber people lived. The only reason they lived together on Ooba was because the white people were forced out of their planet by the Clud. There were probably 150 white rubber villagers with guns against what seemed like 500 Jubi. They were probably 200 yards away, but they were gaining ground, and the white rubber people were near the edge of their village about to be forced completely out.

Whoom! A giant piece of metal from one of the buildings flew right over my head. If I had hesitated to duck, I would have been dead. I came right behind a couple of white rubber people hiding behind one of the buildings at the edge of the village. They pointed their guns at me and probably would have fired if one of the white rubber men hadn't intervened. "Hold it," he said sternly. The others were hesitant at first, but then they lowered their weapons. They still looked at me like they were confused at what I was doing there, and my expression probably didn't give them any answer. I was just as confused as they were, but there I was. There were blasts all around us and guns being shot in the direction of the Jubi. Thankfully, they didn't pay me much attention because they had other more serious problems to worry about other than a scrawny little Gri like me. The white rubber man had a big bright purple print on the back of his neck. He was the only one with the print which I thought was interesting. It looked like it was branded on him and the skin directly around the mark was still white, but it was bubbly looking like it was seared on. The mark looked like a handprint with a J in the middle of it. I had no idea what that meant, but it didn't look like it was coming off any time soon, or ever.

The Jubi were gaining ground quickly and I could see more and more rubber men being shot down and they were covering the streets with their bodies. There was a Jubi at the other end who appeared to be their leader as he was ordering his men to advance, and he looked bigger and different than the rest of them. He walked up to a white rubber man who was trying to crawl back towards his own kind, and he grabbed him by the leg and lifted him up. He was hanging there upside down when a sword pierced right through his chest. Immediately I was overcome with anger and animosity towards him. He was completely helpless. What did he ever do to him? Why were they even attacking them in the first place? The man put up no resistance and he was gutted faster than a blink of an eye. That seemed to be the last straw because right then the white rubber man with the neck brand called out something that must have been "stop" in his language because I couldn't understand it, but all the white men dropped their weapons and came out of their hiding places.

They herded us into the buildings and had guards around us. The Jubi were surprised to see me there, but they just put me with the white rubber men. We were in groups of about 20 crammed in a little room and there were multiple guards surrounding each building with guns. They were talking about their family members that people saw alive. Sadly, lots of the white rubber people had lost some family members. One white rubber man came over by the white rubber man with the mark on his neck who I happened to be standing by, "Torx," he said without muttering, but only loud enough for him and me to hear, "It's your wife," there was a pause "I saw her lying dead on the ground." Now I see why he wanted to talk quietly because this was bad news and the messenger seemed to be suffering greatly for having to be the one to share this news.

He broke down and collapsed to the floor. "And my son?" Torx said trying to hold back his emotions.

"I didn't see him." Torx seemed to have little hope of his kid being alive considering what just happened to their village and his wife. Still on the ground he spoke up in a deeper, louder voice "This is not the end," he said, and everyone listened up, "We will get revenge."

You would think that waking up from a war-torn village with a bunch of 3-eyed people would be a good thing, but after seeing reality I'd prefer my dream any day. Seeing the Jubi from my dreams in real life was much more terrifying. His stature was twice that of a Mountain Man. His hands were about as big as my head. The knife that was strapped to his side was sheathed thankfully, but the thing had to be a mini sword and not a knife. I knew he knew me because of my dream a couple days prior and he still had his black staff in his hand. He was two feet in front of me with his staff pointed in my face. I was being held by two Lexlands who weren't dressed like most other Lexlands. I figured they didn't work for the government which didn't exactly make me feel any better. We were in a large room that seemed to be like the main floor because I saw the tops of other buildings out the window in my peripheral vision. I couldn't see, however, Macrill, Truue, Del or my mother. Dakool was with this man in my dream, but he was also nowhere to be seen here. I remember seeing the bald spot above the ear on the Jubi and it was still there in reality.

With his staff pointed at me from two feet away and the rest of his body towering over mine, he said, "Ahhh Skade, you just can't seem to stay out of trouble, can you?" his voice even deeper than I remembered in my dream. "I don't know what you're talking about." I responded firmly and confidently; I quickly regretted it though because he gave me a stare that would have ripped my soul out had the two guards not been holding me.

"Who are you anyway, and what do you want with me?" I continued to say.

He had a little chuckle. "I am Abcrack, the creator of Ooba!"

"What's with the staff?" I said. "And what do you want with me?" I repeated "And where are my friends?". He chuckled again which I thought was annoying, but I couldn't do anything about it. He was a lot bigger than me and seemed to be more experienced with life in general considering he had created the planet I was living on. He went on to explain that there was a bounty on my head for the murder of a Jubi. The guy in the coal building turned us in for a handsome reward. He knew that I didn't kill the Jubi somehow, but it gave him an excuse to come after me. The Mountain Men were going to turn us in to him before, but somehow, we managed to escape. He didn't talk too highly of the Mountain Men.

"Those fools." he said. He said we should be grateful that we didn't get caught by the brother of the Jubi who died because he would have killed us right then and there. My companions and my mother were all taken and were to be returned to Jacoby to stand trial for helping a "murderer" like myself escape my punishment. For some reason he went on a little side rant that had nothing to do with my questions or myself. He talked about all the battles and wars he'd won, the planets he had conquered and the creatures he had hunted down and killed. He talked about his life's accomplishments as if to impress me, but I really wasn't in the mood to be in awe by what he had done. He went on to talk about how he lets others pretend they are in charge while they sit in their positions of leadership, but everyone knew he was in charge. "I know all, and nothing happens without me finding out about it," he went on to say, boasting of himself.

So, there I was listening to Abcrack tell me all about himself and the things that he's done when he finally seemed to acknowledge why he hadn't turned me in along with my friends. "The dreamers" he said finally on a more engaging note. "I need your help to get to them."

I think he had more to say, but I interrupted him, "I have no idea who they are or how to get to them." I wasn't lying entirely, I knew of them, but I really had no idea who they were or what they were as a matter of fact, let alone how to find them. All I knew was that they were this group that my mother had told me about that dream, and I can relate to that, but they were something more than that and because of the laws of Ooba they have to stay in hiding.

"Don't lie to me boy!" he shouted. Some saliva flew into my face, and I knew he was not to be messed with. At this point in time, I would prefer being burnt to a crisp by the fiery creature than be with this big Jubi, Abcrack.

"I swear, I have no idea how to find them or who they are." I said confidently yet a little hesitant because a fear of disappointing this Jubi had come over me. "I've only heard about them, but that's the extent of my knowledge." I was going to tell him that my mother would know more than I would, but I feared that they would do some bad stuff to her to get it out of her, so I decided to keep that secret to myself. He asked about how I knew them, but I played it off, talking about the rumors from the street about the dreamers. "Why do you want to find them anyway? What do you want with them?" I continued to ask. I thought for a second that he was going to tell me, but I should have known that once he had no use for me I would be considered useless to him. I still don't know why he thought that I would know about them because I'm sure there's plenty of other people that knew about the dreamers a whole lot better than I did.

For being as experienced as he professed and all, he really didn't seem all that bright. He sent me away with the two guards. They had their hands on me the whole time. We came out of the building and there was a smaller ship waiting for us. There was a pilot and two other Jubi guards inside the ship who came out and got me. I felt like a piece of merchandise just being passed on from one owner to the next and I had no control over what happened. The ramp closed and the doors shut. The two guards inside thankfully had a little more sympathy to loosen my straps around my neck and arms so I could move a little more freely. As soon as they were loose again, they strapped me up to the side of the inside of the ship. I realized why they had loosened my straps momentarily, they needed them loose so they could put on different straps is all. "Well, this is great." I thought. At least I was facing a window so I could see outside. I saw all the people who were staring at me as I was put on the ship. Some of them had confused looks on their faces and others seemed to express pity for me. Most of them however basically said with their faces, "You deserve what's coming," and like a spit in my face type thing. For a very brief second I was grateful I was on the ship and not outside with all the people. My legs were strapped separately in these little holes that seemed to fit my feet perfectly. My legs weren't going any-where. My arms were separated and put into two different holes and strapped in so I couldn't move them. I could barely twist my head around so I could see the guards.

"We're good back here," one of the guards said to the pilot. The pilot took off and had I not been strapped down I would have fallen for sure. The Jubi guards didn't fall because of their suctioned feet. "What the?" I accidentally said out loud, hopefully they didn't hear me I thought. "What did you say?" said a guard as if he was offended, I'd opened my mouth. He came towards me and looked like he was about to hit me in the back, but the other guard told him to let it go. First off, I don't know why the guard would be offended by talking, and second, I don't know why the other guard would stick up for me. The other guard though, there was something different about him. I continued to look at him, but in a way that hopefully he wouldn't find offensive because then he might have to hit me, as well as the first guard. He turned his head as if looking out the front window of the ship and then it hit me. His ear was different. I had seen this ear before. I had no idea what it meant, but I had seen this guy before, only before, he was a Gri.

"Well, this can't be good." I thought. He just kept staring out the front window.

My legs and arms were hurting from the uncomfortable position. I asked them multiple times if they could let me out so I could at least move around for a second, but both times the guards didn't respond. We had only been flying for 10 minutes or so when the guard with the bigger ear eased his look from the front. He looked at me and nodded as if something was about to happen. I figured I wouldn't make it back to Jacoby or wherever we were going because he would kill me before we reached our destination. The other guard would probably be happy to go along with it. I was completely hopeless. He got up from his seat and walked towards the other guard and whispered something in his ear. Well, that's when I thought my life was about to be over. The guard smirked as he looked in my direction and then both of them started walking towards me. They undid my straps and I fell to my face as soon as I was freed. I was weak and my muscles were cramped from being in such an awkward position. The guard helped me up while the guard with the different ear stood in front of me as if he was ready to fight me. "You ready?" he said, and I wasn't.

"Just make it quick," I managed to spit out as my limbs were still weak. The guard behind me was basically holding me up at this point because I couldn't stand on my own. The guard held up his fist and I thought for sure this would not feel good, so I winced and braced myself as he threw his punch. I didn't feel anything, but I was sure he'd swung because I closed my eyes as he was swinging towards me. I heard a loud thump right behind me. I opened my eyes and to my astonishment the guard behind me hit the ground.

"Get the pilot." The Jubi with the bigger ear told me. I didn't argue or have time to process what was happening, but I listened to him as the other guard got up. I didn't see it, but I heard the two Jubi guards start fighting and yelling at each other.

"What's going on?" the one guard said who got hit. The other Jubi just kept attacking him without responding. The pilot must have been deaf or something because he didn't seem to notice anything. I opened the door and then I knew why. There was some wack music playing that must have been used to torture people because it sounded terrible. Imagine bark being rubbed together and that's what it sounded like. Somehow the pilot liked it because he was moving back and forth to the beat. I simply hit him on the back of the head with a club that I found hanging on the door.

If you've ever been in a plane that's going super-fast and then the pilot suddenly decides to stop flying it, then you have a good idea of what kind of situation we were in. It was hard to stay balanced as the ship spiraled towards the ground. I got pushed by the momentum towards the top of the cock pit and cut my arm on the top of the chair on my way up. I tried to go towards the wheel to take control of the ship, but as you can imagine it was very difficult. "Get control of the ship." I heard the guard say from the back as if I wasn't trying to do that already. I struggled to grab the seat to pull myself down which took a tremendous amount of my strength. Thankfully I had some adrenaline kick in because I was tired from everything that had been happening and I haven't had more than a couple hours of relaxation or rest over the past week or so. I could see the ground getting closer and closer as I looked out the front window. The trees were coming at us at an incredible speed. We'd probably only have 15 more seconds before we would crash. Then the guard came in somehow. He had a cut lip, and he was holding his left arm. I forgot he had suctioned feet because he just walked up to the wheel and brought it back to level just before we hit the ground.

"Ow" I groaned as I hit the deck since I wasn't tied down to anything when the ship was brought to normal. "What happened to the other guard?" I asked the new pilot. "Let's just say we won't need to worry about him anymore." Well, that sounded good to me, but I still had my doubts about this guard and who he was and what he was doing. As if reading my thoughts, he opened his mouth.

"I'm not really a Jubi as you might have assumed. I am a Gri like you. I am also a dreamer and I'm to take you to the dreamers. We managed to save Macrill, Truue, and Del, but we couldn't get to your mom in time. She's been taken back to Jacoby. She will be fine." He talked as if he knew my mom or something. How did he know she would be fine? "We'll be there in a little." he said and then went silent. I wasn't done talking with him, and how should I know he's telling the truth and isn't another goon trying to get the reward money for me. Just as that thought crossed my mind, he handed me something.

"Our family necklace!" I said in astonishment. "How did you get this?"

"Your mother." he responded, "She knew you'd need convincing, so she gave it to me."

"Wait, so you saw her. When did she give it to you?" I asked right after. "How'd she not get away then?" My feelings started to boil, and I was getting mad that he had the nerve to get the necklace from her without saving her.

"I know what you're thinking." he said, which didn't surprise me considering he'd read my mind multiple times already, "She said it was necessary to go back to Jacoby." He paused for a second, "We would have rescued her, but she said not to." I didn't know what to think. Why would my mom not escape if she was given the chance to escape? Didn't she know that I needed her? I went towards the back and sat down in one of the seats, holding our family's necklace. It wasn't long before he said, "We've made it!" I ran up to the front to see where we were and what he was talking about. Before I got to the front to see for myself, "Skade," the guard mentioned, "You need to be careful, even here." I didn't know what he was talking about exactly as I came to the front. "And also," he sighed and gave me a faint smile as I entered the cock pit, "Phylaman, Phylaman is my name."

The Truth

If you were expecting a big eloquent looking building full of perfect people, all happy and joyful, then you'd be just as disappointed as I was. There was no big building, and the area that it was in was nothing short of barren. The headquarters were in this small area of smaller buildings right at the base of a big mountain. There seemed to be no greenery anywhere which wasn't completely unnatural for Ooba, but you'd think maybe there'd still be something green. The city seemed very small, but it was bigger than a village. There was a big cave looking thing at the back. "That's where we're headed." Phylaman said, pointing towards the cave. It was dark in there and it looked like our entire ship could fit inside of it. We flew our ship to the middle of the city where there were some landing pads and we headed towards the base of the mountain where the big cave was. There were lots of different races here, but there were more Gri than any other race. I didn't know why that was or if that was a good thing or not, but it's what it was. Nobody seemed to pay us much attention, which I assumed meant that they had lots of people come and go so we were no different. Well, I guess up to that point I didn't think I was any different anyway, but sometimes people thought I was different for some odd reason. The unofficial ruler of Ooba, and its creator Abrack, seemed to believe that I was important. Truue came to rescue us from the Mountain Men because he knew something about us that we didn't. I guess I'm a little slow on who I am or my importance, but I tried not to think about it. I was still convinced that they were probably thinking of the wrong guy. We started to make our way when I noticed something very strange.

"What are these people doing?" I asked Phylaman wearily. I was a little bit afraid for the people around us.

He chuckled and gave me a smile. "Things are different here." he said simply. I didn't appreciate how he could never just give me a straightforward simple answer. It was weird, a lot of the people we were passing had ripped eyes. Yeah, they were ripped, as in they had been dreaming. They were walking around in broad daylight, well I guess that is always the case here on Ooba, but still. Were they not afraid of getting caught? Don't they know the rules? What if someone ratted them out?

"I told you," Phylaman said as if reading my thoughts, "things are different here. Do you remember what I told you about this place?" He then asked me.

"Um, yeah, I remember you saying that." I said. I guess that wasn't the answer he was looking for because he gave me a disappointed look. "No, remember that you still have to be careful around here." He said quietly. "Oh yeah." I responded having completely forgotten that until he just mentioned it again. "But why?" and as soon as I said it, I wished I hadn't. His look made me feel dumb and unintelligent for asking such a dumb question. Also, I said it a little louder than he wanted, because he kept looking around at the others around him as if expecting them to react or do something for talking loudly. Thankfully nothing happened and we kept walking.

It was astonishing how many people we passed with ripped eyes. It was a little relieving in the sense that I wasn't the only one dreaming, but there were tons of others dreaming as well, and they must have been proud of it because they were out in the open. After passing through a couple of streets and houses we came to the big cave. Did I say it was big already? Man, this thing was huge. From a distance it was big, but up close it could have fit 10 of our little ships in here. That little fiery monster that we encountered back in the mountains was nothing compared to the size of this cave. There was a cool breeze that was coming out of it, and it felt so good.

"Skade!" I heard someone with a familiar voice say somewhere inside the cave. It was a little darker in the cave than outside, which wasn't hard to do, but then I saw him. Macrill came running out of the cave with Del and Truue right behind him. This was a very happy sight, but then I remembered that my mom wasn't there. Some feelings of guilt and sadness came over me, but I tried not to show it. "She'll be fine." Phylaman said as he patted my shoulder and motioned me to go meet my friends. I ran towards them and gave them all a big hug.

"You guys are okay." I said cheerfully as we embraced. "I was so worried." I continued to say, "I'm glad we're back together." They all seemed happy to see me, but they also seemed too confident almost, like they weren't that worried at all.

"We knew it would work," Del said.

"Uh" I started to pull back from the embrace, "What do you mean? You knew it would work."

"Yeah, we knew it would work." Truue chimed in.

"Alrighty," I said, "You guys got some explaining to do, and I need to know everything."

Macrill has never been good at telling stories and remembering important details, so I didn't exactly understand everything that happened. What I got out of it was they got taken, got rescued somehow, except my mother. He mentioned that multiple times as if I didn't know that, considering she wasn't with us. Then they magically made it to the headquarters and have been here ever since. I tried to look at Truue or Del for more information or clarification, but they couldn't seem to keep themselves together after hearing the story told by Macrill. It was useless, I thought. Anyway, we were all back together, well for the most part, and that was good.

We headed into the cave to find out what this whole dreaming society was about. The cave was very wide, but there were lots of rocks on the base near the sides of the cave so there wasn't a lot of walking room. There were lots of protrusions of rocks sticking out in all directions that you only saw as you entered the cave. It seemed that the number of weird shaped rocks sticking out of the walls and the ground increased as we went into the cave. The ground was very hard. There was a little breeze coming through the cave that felt good. The smell was normal, but you could tell it was different. It was a little more humid inside the cave than it was outside. We were the only people going into or out of the cave. Multiple times we had to move over as a group of people were coming out. We passed a lot of Gri. It seemed that every race was represented in the cave, but there were more Gri than anybody. I didn't know if I should be nervous or not about all the Gri here because the government might single us out even more than they already did. The Jubi let us into Ooba because we were desperate, but frankly I don't think they've ever expressed their true feelings about us being here. I don't think they respected us since we got here, and it hasn't changed. All the Jubi probably think that we're all dreamers and that we're up to no good and we're looking to overthrow them somehow. As far as I knew the Gri were happy to be here as long as it was away from the Clud. With regards to the dreamers and their motives I have no idea what they're wanting. Also, I can't really speak for them considering I'm not even part of their little group. To my surprise their group was not that little.

The random rocks forming along the sides and base of the wall stopped suddenly and the pathway opened to the size of the cave. The cave wasn't entirely pitch black, but there was definitely more light coming from the direction we were headed. We heard some voices in the distance. As we got closer, we found ourselves in this large corridor full of people talking amongst themselves. I looked up and found large holes in the cave that let light and a draft through the cave. The cave seemed to keep going, but I had a feeling that this would be as far as we would ever need to go. Also, why we needed to meet in a cave of all places was beyond me. There was a man in the middle of all the races.

"Skade." shouted the man in the middle as soon as he saw me. "Come forward." I had no idea how all these people knew my name and why'd they want anything to do with me.

Macrill nudged me in the back, "Well go on," he said. I trudged forward slowly as all the chatter in the room went silent. I didn't see everyone looking at me, but I could feel their gaze. I approached the Gri who called my name out. I didn't recognize him, but he looked like he was the leader. There was a confidence about him and a certain look that he had that just radiated leadership. He was a little bigger than I was. He was wearing a cut-up protective suit, revealing his arms that were twice the size of mine. He's not the kind of Gri you want to start a fight with. His eyes were ripped. The part of his skin where the protective suit had been ripped was a little bubble like from a burn, but it didn't seem to faze him. He was probably immune to pain. He had a big gun strapped to his back. The point of it was about half a foot above his head. He held his arms out to embrace me as I came forward, he had a big red scar under his arm that seemed to run along his side, but it was covered by his protective suit. This dude had been through some tough stuff.

"We're glad you made it." he said as he about suffocated me with a mountain man like hug. His strength was unbearable.

"Glad to be here," I choked out, as the air went out of me. I thought he was going to hug me to death, but he finally let me go after a bit. He patted me on the shoulder and raised my arm up.

"Skade, son of Tekrum." Everyone erupted into cheers and stomping. I was still trying to catch my breath, so I probably didn't look very firm or confident, thinking about it even with my breath I didn't look confident anyway. They didn't seem to care or mind as they shouted and stomped. The man lowered my arm and then spoke to everyone, "We will adjourn our discussion until tomorrow. Until then, rest up." He waved them away and they all started heading back to the village outside the cave. As everyone had left but a handful of us. We headed to a table that I hadn't seen before with all the people covering it. There were multiple tables around the corridor and the table we went to didn't look any different or special compared to the others. Macrill, Del, the Gri in charge and I all sat down. Truue was standing right behind us as were a couple of other people I didn't recognize. "Well, Skade, son of Tekrum," the Gri said, "we have much to talk about."

What was shared with me was hard to believe and very shocking. When people somehow know your name, whom you've never met before suddenly think that you're the answer to all their problems is not easy to process or handle. I was still trying to take in the fact that the creator of Ooba knew of me and tried to get information out of me about a group I didn't know about. Just after that I was rescued from him by the group that I didn't know anything about. The dreaming society somehow knew about me, and their leader knew my name and was now trying to tell me all sorts of stuff. It was a lot to take in. Their leader, the guy who was talking to me was Wroff. He had been here on Ooba for a little longer than I had been. He was a lot older than me. He went on to tell me how he created the dreaming society. Their purpose was to honor their traditions and their innate abilities to dream. They believe that nobody should take that from them, with which I completely agree. The next part came as a big shock to me, however, he said that my dad was alive.

How can it be? I was there when the Clud attacked our home planet, and we were forced out. My dad risked his life for me to escape. So many thoughts and emotions were going through me. Wroff recognized this and let me take it in before he continued to talk. If he were alive how would Wroff know about it, and I wouldn't? What has my dad been doing all these years while we were here on Ooba? Macrill put his arm around me and squeezed. I wanted to break out into tears, but the tears never came. With all the emotions that I was feeling I couldn't seem to "feel" like it was real or possible.

After a minute Wroff continued, "We need to stop Abrack. He is plotting to annihilate everyone on Ooba except the Jubi with the help of the Clud. Your dad may have found a way to cure the Clud. Abrack has somehow known this and wants you to help him get to your father for reasons you may guess." He took a breath; it was a lot to talk about. "I know that this is a lot for you to take in, but it's the truth. I know you have lots of questions, but things will make more sense with time. If you search deep down, you will know that what I am telling you is true." I just sat there listening. I couldn't find it in me to look at him and I just kept my eyes focused on the ground just next to me.

Just then we heard some sirens going off outside the cave. My mind was completely taken off what was just shared with me by Wroff. Everyone seemed to get an anxious look on their faces. They all headed towards the exit. Outside there were people gathered all around in the streets looking in the direction of a larger ship coming in. The ship landed right in the middle of this big open area I had failed to see before. It seemed to be the only place in the village that wasn't full of buildings and houses. The people seemed to crowd the ramp way as soon as the ship landed. "What's going on?" I leaned over to Macrill.

"I don't know." He said. There was a bonging in the air and then the ramp came down. People flooded out of the ship. There seemed to be 80 or so of them. The ship was very big and based off the markings on the ship it had been through a lot. There were some gashes and giant holes in the ship, and it creaked a lot when the ramp lowered. I figured the ship had seen better days, but this just instilled a greater curiosity to know where the ship and its members had come from. There were lots of happy reunions between the people in the village and the people coming off the ship as I assumed they were probably family. The people looked beat up and very tired. Some of them had injuries all over their bodies. There were a few lucky ones who didn't seem to have more than two abrasions or bruises. I noticed Wroff go towards the crew and a Gri handed him some necklaces and I saw his sad expression. Those were probably from their comrades who didn't make it, I thought. There were some people coming down last carrying others in beds. There was somebody in a bed that looked familiar. I was far off on top of a building to get a better view. Macrill seemed to notice what I was looking at and had a similar thought. It was hard to tell for certain because we were so far off and couldn't see for certain. "It can't be." Macrill gasped. "Can it?" I didn't answer him, but instead ran off towards the ship so I could get a close-up view for myself.

"How could this be?" I thought. "Was it really her? I thought she was killed long ago. It's not possible, is it?"

Down in the streets I realized there were way more people than I had seen up in the building. It was hard to make my way in a quick manner. I had to push and squeeze my way through while Macrill was right behind me. I seemed to lose him a couple times, but he always managed to find me again. As I got closer to the ship, I saw some of the people who came off the ship and recognized them from their wounds. They all seemed to be rejoicing and happy that they were together again. There were some beat up people. I wondered where they had been and what had happened to them.

There were so many people, I was beginning to get frustrated. The suns were at their optimal point for our village, making it even hotter outside than at other hours of the day. "Skade," I managed to hear somebody yell out from ahead of me. I tried looking for where the voice was coming from exactly. I noticed it was Macrill, so I yelled back. He was standing on top of a bench looking around and we made eye contact. I made my way towards him. He was talking to a man who seemed to have come off the ship. "In that building over there" he said as he pointed to one of the bigger buildings in the village. "This way." Macrill said as we headed towards the building. I tried asking him about the building and why we needed to go there, but there was a lot of noise around so we couldn't exactly communicate properly. We got split up once again through the crowd. They seemed to be very aggressive and almost rude like since the ship came in. Everyone was racing around wildly trying to find their loved ones. It was hard to lose sight of the building so at least I knew which direction to head. I still didn't know why we were headed towards the building, but I wasn't having any luck of finding her in the crowd.

The doors opened and there was a cool breeze that went across my skin. There were lots of bodies on the floor. These bodies seemed to have gotten the worst of it. There was lots of blood and what looked like multiple people running around trying to help the wounded. I scanned the room quickly looking for Macrill. I was walking through the people trying not to step on any of them or get in the way of the people doing the healing. I saw things that I wouldn't wish anybody to go through or let alone see. Back near the corner of the room I saw her. I quickly made my way over weaving through people and came up to her side. She wasn't moving and her eyes were shut. She had a big gash over her left arm and a bandage wrapping around her neck. "Tide" I muttered.

Discussing with most of the group that had come back healthy to the cave was quite enlightening. They talked about the state of multiple other worlds in other galaxies who were dealing with the Clud. These Clud just seemed totally invincible, and nothing was known to stop them let alone slow them down. One guy was talking about a world full of huts in some marshes which caught my attention because he described a place I had seen in my dreams. The Clud were beginning to invade their world, but there were lots of hideouts that made it difficult for the Clud to find them. There were still some safe areas in that world, but who knows how much longer they will be safe. There was another man who talked about this world full of water and there were floating landmarks and buildings where the Clud had attacked. Some of the sea monsters on that world had managed to fend off some of the Clud which the people recognized, so they submerged themselves with their crafts while the Clud were attacking. The sea creatures weren't the friendliest towards the people either however, so they had to watch where they were going. He barely managed to survive while he was protected by some of the people of that world. His vessel was attacked by the Clud ships just before they submerged, and they were left alone by the Clud because they didn't want to get attacked by a sea creature if they came for them. We were in the water for 20 minutes when we saw from the distance a scaly back just peek out of the water. Just before it got to them another ship came from below and dragged me down with it just before the creature got my crew mates. The crew mates let me go and they went down with the creature.

There were plenty of stories like that. Talking about the Clud and their destruction of the universe. Wroff was at the front listening to all the stories and seemed almost calm like he knew everything in the first place. "How could he be so calm?" I thought. "Why would so many people risk their lives to save these dreamers? Why would the dreamers leave Ooba to go check out other worlds if they knew it wasn't safe?" There were lots of questions that I had going through my head. The group gathered together was down in spirit and there seemed to be little hope. Truue was next to me, and he had a look about him as if a Clud were standing right in front of him.

"We still haven't found Tekrum." Shouted somebody from the crowd.

"The Clud invaded my planet and left nobody alive." Spoke another voice.

"Dakool and the government aren't accepting our terms."

"Wait. What terms?" I thought. There was a lot of news that I had taken in over the last couple days and this one caught me off guard the most. I was still trying to process the idea that my father and sister were both alive, but what terms were we trying to get the government to agree on? There's still unrest in Jacoby and other areas because of my escape. There seems to be unrest and tension in most cities and our reputation as dreamers is declining in a negative way. There were lots of comments and things that I was trying to wrap my mind around. I knew Ooba was big and the universe was infinitely bigger, but it really hit different when all these problems seemed so relevant to so many people who had my same intentions and motives.

There was a lot going on and a lot of new things to take in which was starting to become part of my life. It seemed like everyone around me knew what was going on and how things were going except for me. Attending this meeting just made me more confused at everything that's been happening. My dad was still alive as was my sister, who I thought were both dead. My mother, who I've been with since birth was now about to get executed for all I knew.

"What's that for?" I asked as I heard the sirens coming from outside the cave once again. I just got a shrug from Del and Macrill who also looked as surprised as I was. Everyone in the room who was in the discussion started to run outside, but they looked nervous. I didn't know what the sirens were sounding off for, but they couldn't be good.

As we ran towards the entrance of the cave we were hit by the heat. Even after living on Ooba for years now, I still forget just how hot it is. You didn't realize just how much of a difference the cave cooled you off. There seemed to be people running in all sorts of directions with their protective gear on. Most of them had bags thrown over their shoulders. I was a little behind Wroff who was listening to one of the guards just outside the cave. I couldn't see his face, but I had a feeling he had a surprised look on it by the way he threw his hands above his head and the gasp he let out.

"What is it?" I asked from behind. He turned towards me, and his face confirmed what I had thought.

"We got to move. The Lexlands are coming for us." I had only been here for a couple days and already I was being asked to flee. I shouldn't be surprised though considering that's how most of my life has gone anyway. I never have too much time to settle in and make a place a new home.

We bolted down into the main streets where everyone else was running frantically. We headed towards the building to find my sister. I wasn't about to leave her to be taken and I knew nobody else would want to drag her along, she'd slow them down. We entered the building after wading through the crowd of people outside. The inside seemed even worse. It seemed like all the injured people were being taken by the workers. I ran back towards the corner where Tide was resting before, but there was nobody there. Her mat was still there though. "Where is she?" Macrill said.

"I don't know." I replied, trying to stay calm. "We will have to find her," I said, trying to be optimistic and hopeful, "She can't be too far" We headed back out after adjusting our suits quickly as they usually loosen the more, we move. There were less people in the streets, but there were lots of ships taking off from all around the city. A lot of people had their ships above their buildings, any-where else they would just be in the way, considering how small our little village was.

"I'll go find Wroff and a ship while you guys keep looking for Tide. Let's meet up above the cave in 20 minutes," Macrill said. Del, Truue and I all looked at each other and nodded. I went back towards the center of the village hoping to find her while Del and Truue both went in different directions. Thankfully, there were not as many people running through the streets as there were before.

"They're going to make it." I thought to myself. That was the fastest 20 minutes of my life. I had no luck in finding my sister, but I still had hope that one of my friends had found her and she was okay. The streets were practically empty. I assumed these people had been booted from past homes just like this and they were used to it by now. It didn't take them long to leave once the word was out. I wondered where they would go though. Would everyone just go off on their own trying not to get caught. It was a sad feeling, in that everyone had to leave so abruptly because they weren't allowed to live how they did in past worlds. I got upset with Abrack and Dakool for what they were doing and wanted revenge. It was a faint hope because I knew I was in no position to get any sort of revenge. I saw a ship up above the cave. I made my way up around the mountain along a little trail that was there. Macrill was down at the bottom of the ramp. "No luck." I thought as I saw his hopeful expression die down as he saw me alone. "Where was Tide?"

Our ship was full of people. The engines must have been heavy duty to carry a load like we had. I was sitting down near the back next to Macrill and I glanced at everyone on our shuttle. There must have been 30 people crammed into our little ship and they all looked so sad and depressed. It was quiet. Nobody seemed to move, and everyone just looked distraught.

We seemed to head in the opposite direction of Bagger. There were a lot of deserted buildings that we passed over. I didn't know what city we were above, but it was completely desolate. We didn't see any movement anywhere. There weren't even any creatures or animals in the city, it was abandoned for sure. I wondered what had happened to it and where everyone had gone, but I didn't give it much thought. We came across a large body of water that was surrounded by sand as far as I could tell. It looked like the water was bubbling at some points. The water must have been hot. We saw some weird looking creatures on the edge of the water in the sand, they were getting a drink. I didn't know how it wasn't burning them. There were some large shadows moving near the top of the water and I thought that was even more bizarre. I don't know how any creature could survive in that.

"We're almost there," said somebody from up at the front of our craft. I didn't recognize the voice and it got me thinking of how many people are actually part of this dreaming society that I didn't know about. Seeing all the people back at our old location was eye opening, but right then it really hit me that there were so many people who were sacrificing their lives for the society. Dreamers were from all over and from all types of races. Some races obviously had more dreamers such as the Gri, while others had very few dreamers. I wondered why that was and how it came to be like that. These were questions that made me really think and it took up all my focus. I didn't realize how long I had been in that train of thought with these questions swirling through my head when I heard other ships outside of our own flying by us. I looked out the window and saw another mountain that had a cave entrance halfway up to the top.

"What was it with these guys and caves?" I thought. The mountain wasn't as big as the last, but it looked like there were already people heading toward the cave.

We landed our ship and Wroff told everyone on our ship to head for the cave. "What about my sister?" I asked him on my way off the ship.

"We will find her, I'm sure of it." He responded, "Just head for the cave for now. We have a special ceremony to perform."

"A special ceremony?" I said under my breath. I just wanted to find my sister and now I'm finding out we have to do some special ceremony.

We Meet a Catcher

This cave was a little smaller than the last cave we were in, but it had a very interesting layout. There were lots of smaller, hall-like spaces carved out of the rock leading to smaller rooms. If you were expecting a big giant room like the last cave, then you'd be off. It was like a giant maze and without the help of the drawings on the walls everybody would get lost. The mountain wasn't as big as the last mountain either, so it was a little surprising to see just how endless the cave seemed to be. There were small rooms and big rooms alike. The ceiling in some areas was very low to the ground while in others the ceiling was well above 20 feet. There were almost naturally occurring steps in some parts of the cave. There must have been multiple floors to the cave, and I was willing to bet that there was more than one entrance and exit from the cave, unlike our last cave that just had the one entrance and exit. After following some dreamers who knew the cave better, we arrived at a smaller room where it was significantly cooler than the other parts of the cave. Macrill, Del, and Truue and I peeked in and saw that it wouldn't fit all of us in that room. Wroff was already in there somehow, even though we entered the cave before him. He looked at us with a calm expression, "I'll start with Skade." A lump formed in my throat because I still had no idea what this ritual was all about, and I was still worrying about my sister. There had been no news or sign of her here at our new headquarters. There was a big pad on top of a protruding rock that he had me sit on. There was a small black hole right at the center of the wall to my left where cold air was spewing in. I wondered how this hole formed so perfectly to provide natural cool air and where it was coming from exactly, but I didn't ask. It felt good though. "You've dreamed others dreams before, yes?" Wroff asked me.

"Uh yeah." I responded skeptically because I didn't know if it was a trick question or not. I felt like every dreamer has dreamed another's dream before. I remember when I was first learning about my dreaming abilities, my father would put his hand on my arm, and he'd help me understand my own dreams and help me be able to read and interpret them. This was a happy thought, and I remembered at that moment that somehow, he was still alive. My mind went back in time during one of my first experiences of dreaming with my father.

I was in a body that didn't feel like my own. There was a little familiarity with the body however that intrigued me. I was in a room laying on my bed and it was very dark. I got out of my bed and headed outside. Outside was dark except for the blue lights coming off the street poles. I seemed to be the only one outside. It was completely quiet besides some groans from animals from the forest behind the house. I looked down at my hands and my feelings were confirmed, this was not my body. I couldn't see my face, but my body was definitely thicker. I felt like I had gained a hundred pounds. I felt like I was a prime meal for some of the creatures in the forest. I would be a good breakfast for a Yikee, but he'd need to eat double me to feed him for the day. After considering my new body I was in, I heard an odd sound coming from the forest. It wasn't the smartest thing to do looking back at it, but I made my way towards the forest to see what the sound was. It was very hard to see more than 5 feet in front of me and it wasn't safe going into the forest alone during the later part of the day. Most of the creatures who could eat Gri were active at night. There was some thick brush and lots of roots sticking out. I stumbled a couple times, but I continued forwards, pausing every once in a while, to listen to the noise I was hearing. It sounded like a rubber ball was being squeezed out of a cracking tree. I tried to watch my step and make as little noise as possible because I didn't want to draw any attention from any other creature in the area. For whatever reason I wasn't afraid of approaching this noise, thinking that it wouldn't be out to get me, unlike other creatures in the forest. I made it fifty yards into the forest and then I saw it directly in front of me. I have heard of these animals, but I thought they were legends. They are big six-legged creatures, but only four legs ever touch the ground at the same time. They have three legs on each side that spin off a joint protruding from the side of the torso. They have a normal looking bird head without the eyes. They have a big beak and wings that can come out of the front and the back. They fly in the opposite direction from which they walk. They have three long and roughly two inches thick antennas that come down their head that connect back to the top of their head. They are only visible to those who are within fifty yards of them. As of ten seconds ago these creatures were only legends in my mind, but now I know.

He was bleeding out of two of his legs on his left side. I slowly approached him hoping that I could further assess the damage. As I got closer, I instinctively put my hand on his extended wing in the front and closed my eyes.

It was like I could feel the pain the Krock was going through. I saw what had happened to it and I could feel his emotions. I concentrated on the wounds and as I did so I felt relief. The pulse of the creature began to slow, and the breathing calmed down. I was healing the Krock. The feeling was surreal, and it was something that I had never experienced before. I knew then that I had the ability to heal. "Would all dreamers have these abilities?" I thought. "Was there a limit to these powers?" After 3 minutes with my arm on the wing, I let go. The Krock stood up on 4 of his legs, two on each side and I realized just how big it was. It doubled my size when I was standing up. I didn't feel endangered, but then something else sounded off behind us and the Krock tensed up. I turned toward where the noise was coming from and saw a Notsl headed straight at me. A Notsl is a creature that will eat Gri. It came over me quicker than I had time to react. Just before it was on top of me, however, the Krock sprang on the Notsl and then I woke up. That's when I learned that I could heal others. My father said afterward that not all dreamers can heal others, but most can. All dreamers can interpret others dreams though.

"Hello, Skade? You there?" Wroff asked me.

"Oh yeah, sorry. I'm good." I responded. I was lying a little though, that experience took me back into a trance and then I thought about how my father might know how to heal the Clud.

"Okay, for this to work you need to lay down and I will put my hand on your arm, and I will show you what we do." he told me. I closed my eyes and laid down. His hand was very rough and tough. If I had to guess without seeing him, I would have thought he was a Jubi because his hands were workers hands. That thought quickly faded as a new scene appeared in my mind. I was with other dreamers in a big room surrounded by Lexlands with weapons in their hands. I stood up and my mouth opened, but it didn't feel like it was mine. I knew Wroff was with me, so he was probably acting in my place. The Lexlands made their way through the other dreamers and grabbed me. They carried me off and I was taken out into the streets where a large group was gathered. I saw my parents and my sister along with Macrill in the front being held back by some guards. My mom was crying, and my father was trying to plead his case to the guards to let me go and take him instead. At that moment I was left to myself. Wroff had left and it was up to me to decide.

"No father," I said. "I will go". I didn't even know what was happening, but I didn't want my father or anybody else to suffer, even if I didn't do anything. The guards obviously didn't listen to me and took me towards my family and threw me at my mother who embraced me, and we both fell backwards. They took my father and started dragging him away. "NOOO," I shouted as I got off the ground with my mother still embracing me. She had a confused look on her face. I pried her off of me and pushed my way past the guards who were trying to hold me back, but I wasn't going to let them stop me. "I said take me." I got right in the face of one of the guards holding my dad and he just smirked and let my father go. My mother started sobbing even more. I turned towards her and smiled and mouthed "It'll be okay." And then I woke up.

"Interesting," Wroff whispered.

"Um, what? What was that all about?" I asked.

"The purpose of the ritual was to see how much we were willing to sacrifice for the benefit of the dreamers and others who aren't at fault. We get put in situations where it is hard to sacrifice, in your case you had to take the place of your father when everyone knows that the father is always most willing to take the blame to protect the family. You did a good job Skade, the best I have ever seen." He paused then continued, "I knew you were special, so I skipped a lot of the other little tests knowing that you would pass them, but that one that you experienced was the most crucial of them all and not many people pass them. Being willing to sacrifice for others, especially a parent who would take your place, when you know that it's better that you suffer than have somebody else who may be an innocent sufferer. Your genes are special, and we will rely on you heavily if we are to survive the Clud and stay here on Ooba."

I was taken to a room to rest. As you know, people who dream usually wake up extra tired and they itch, and the eyes are ripped as they call it here on Ooba. "My genes were different." I thought. I knew everyone was different, but this hit different. I felt like I had a greater purpose though I still felt like I was this incapable little kid. I got thinking about how my dad might have figured out a way to somehow capture a Clud; get him to calm down, and then somehow heal them. That was a lot of wishful thinking. The universe could be so different. "Could we go back to Zazri and live in our home world? What would our home world be like now that it's been invaded by the Clud. Would they still be there? Would there have been any survivors? How long would it take to heal the Clud? There were a lot of Clud. Would they stay healed permanently or would they revert back to their old ways? Would they have the same tendencies?"

So many questions were swirling through my head. My eyes itched and I felt super tired. Usually, the ripped eyes and the weariness leaves after a little. I felt like I was in the resting room longer than normal because of all the questions I was considering. "Was it really possible?"

I got off my elevated pad that was concealed in the back in one of the cave rooms. Macrill was just outside the room. I think he heard me get up and then peeked in. I was still a little tired, but I was good enough to leave. "Skade." Macrill said as if trying to hide something as he looked at me. "It's your sister. We've found her." My whole focus shifted.

"Is she okay? Where is she at?"

"Yeah, she seems to be okay, but she needs to be rescued."

"What do you mean rescued?"

"Well, her ship crashed as they were making their way around the city of Aboo."

"Wait Aboo, Aboo? As in the city that basically is full of catchers, and they follow all the rules of Ooba to a T?"

"Unfortunately, yes that city." Macrill went on to say, "And somehow before they left their ship, they sent us a message that just barely got through and they need transportation. Their ship is irreparable."

"How much time do you think they'll have before they get noticed?" I asked.

"I would guess, half a day tops. We'll need to leave right now if we're to get them out."

Finding a ship that was ready to take off right away was a little difficult. After our long flight from our last place all the ships were under maintenance and being cleaned and re-fueled. Thankfully, there was a smaller ship that wasn't being worked on and it didn't require too many people to pilot it. The pilot of the ship was just finishing putting away the oil tubes and he said he'd take us. Funny thing about Ooba is in most places outside of the big city usually it's not too hard to find oil. Oil seeps through the ground here because there is so much of it on Ooba. I don't know how they managed to bring in all this oil onto this planet when they created it, but I wasn't complaining. Sometimes you just had to watch your step because the oil would typically be very hot, and it would burn on contact. Basically, the pilot just dropped the oil tubes on the oily puddle as soon as he agreed to help us. His ship was a little newer and it was very fast. We were still a way away from Aboo so we tried to come up with some type of plan in the meantime. We didn't make it very far before Macrill and I were both distracted as we flew on the outskirts of Jacoby. We hadn't been gone for too long and the city looked completely different. It didn't look like it was doing good. Ever since that murder in the fields the city just never got better I guessed. There were some small flames coming out of one of the buildings near the center part of the city. It was a little hard to be certain because we were a way off, but it didn't look like it was the building we lived in. I secretly hoped it was a building that was home to the Lexland government guard, but I knew too well it wouldn't still be burning if that were the case. Things can get out of hand fast here on Ooba, but somehow the government buildings were usually the most protected and it was hard to do anything about it.

My eye caught something small near the back of our ship. It was small at first, but it grew quickly, and it sped towards us. There were two ships that were on our tail just as we flew out of sight of Jacoby. Our pilot started talking, but it wasn't to Macrill or me as we were both in the back. We approached him and could pick out, "allowed to fly." said a voice coming from the communication system up front. "That will not be necessary" Our pilot replied, "We are simply traveling to Aboo." "Why'd you need to fly so close to Jacoby?" a voice said. "We're supposed to keep the skies clear until things settle down."

"Our apologies, our pilot said, we were unaware of any such demands as our communication systems have been broken until just recently."

"And nobody at Bagger let you know of our recent demands?"

"Bagger." I thought. He must have told them we were coming from Bagger. Things might get a little serious if we're not careful.

"No," our pilot responded, "I told you our communications were down until after we left." "We will be sure not to fly back anywhere near the city on our return."

"Make sure of it." The system sounded back firmly. "We'll let you slide this time, but make sure to fly far away from Jacoby on your way back." The system went quiet, and we were now close enough to see the pilot as he wiped away some sweat from his head with deep relief.

"That was close," he said as if he knew we were there behind him.

"Well, Macrill," I said. "Back to planning how we're going to get in and out safely."

Aboo was nothing like any other city I have been in. For some reason I assumed Aboo would be like the other bigger cities; full of bigger modern buildings where the citizens would reside. Even a little greenery or mountains on the outskirts of the city with some main roads leading out in their direction. My assumptions were off just a little. Here in Aboo they had a big open desert around their city. There were big fences that only had a few runways for ships to come in. And a couple pathways for small vehicles or people to walk through. This city was completely secured from who knows what. It seemed as if they were preparing for all the citizens on Ooba to attack them. I wonder who had the final say in the city's defenses and layout. I don't know how my sister got in here without raising any suspicion. I don't know how we were going to get in there safely and be able to leave without raising any alarms or trouble.

We landed our ship just outside of the security tunnel that led into the city. We saw hundreds of other ships that had touched down on the desert floor and some had covers while others didn't. With time, ships tend to take a toll from the two stars around Ooba, so the wealthier people had covers for their ships to last longer. We found a little flat piece of ground where we landed our ship. You could feel the heat as soon as we opened the ship doors. There was no wind and it felt extra hot here for whatever reason. Even in our protective gear the heat was almost too much to bear.

The security gates where people were walking in and out of were no more secure than the ship doors. There were long lines, but they seemed to be moving very quickly. There was a big gate at the end that seemed to open every twenty seconds for about twenty seconds and then it would close again. As we got closer, I saw there were two separate lines of people. The big doors let in groups at a time who just scanned a little card that must have been a resident card. Then there was another smaller door that opened and closed just long enough for one person to get through after being asked questions by security guards. The other line was a residential line, and our line had a big sign that said "Foreigners". "What are they being asked do you think?" Macrill leaned over to me and asked.

"I have no idea," I replied. Our pilot who was also with us piped in, "They are just asking basic questions regarding our intended interest in entering their city and how long we will be staying."

"Oh." Macrill and I both said at the same time as if all would be okay then. "It's not like we were dreamers or wanted by the government in other parts of Ooba, but yeah we should be good." I thought, trying to convince myself that we would be okay. We approached the men as the line shrank and we were all separated and interviewed separately. Surprisingly the interview went quickly, and they didn't seem too suspicious with any of my answers. They pointed me in the direction of the door. Still confused that it went so easily I was hesitant at first to go towards the door, but then I realized that would draw more attention, so I tried to go as normal as possible. The gate slid open for the person in front of me. The guard motioned me forward to the gate. It closed as soon as the person in front of me went through. The guard pointed me to go through when the door opened, but I wasn't paying too much attention. I was trying to scan behind me and in the other lines to see if I could see our pilot or Macrill. I heard the door open, but I didn't move.

"Hey!" The guard said sternly, "You better go through." I slowly walked through and as soon as my left foot got past, the door slammed shut.

There were so many people. Some were waiting 15 feet past the door, waiting for others to get through. I was pushed from behind, I stumbled to not fall down. I turned, the Lexland behind me was one of the biggest I have ever seen, but he was missing an eye and his metal framed body seemed like it was charred from some fire. "Better watch yourself kid." he mentioned in a deep voice. He just walked right past me. Another hand was put on my arm, and I turned to see who it was.

"Glad you made it," I said, "Where's Macrill?" I spoke softly trying not to throw his name around. Who knows who would be looking for us in this city.

"I don't know" he replied, "I thought he was with you. I saw him right behind you just before I went in."

We spent the next 5 minutes frantically looking around while somehow trying to not draw attention to ourselves. Everybody just seemed so calm and relaxed in this place. There was a ship station that took the people to different parts of the city. There were vendors that all seemed very happy and content selling their goods and trades. I got a glimpse of the back side of Macrill headed in the opposite direction of me. It seems as if he was also looking for us. I didn't want to call out to him fearing that there would be people who would be looking for us, to turn us in. Even since being close to the dreaming society things have felt different after Abrack put a reward up for us. I quickened my pace and put my hand on his elbow. He was startled and almost swung at me until he realized it was me. "It's okay, it's okay" I said, trying to comfort him.

"Oh," he sighed, "they took me to a separate entrance as soon as we got split up and I thought I wasn't going to get out of there. The guards and security here are way better than anywhere we've been, that's for sure".

"Yeah, it seems that that is the case" I replied. "We'll have to be extra careful here." I whispered quietly as I turned to find the pilot coming in our direction.

We took the next ship into the downtown area. The buildings here were made up of the desert sand which I thought was wild considering desert sand typically does not compact well. The buildings were all dome shaped and they seemed to be pretty empty. With how many people we saw coming into the city and how big it was I wondered why the inner part of the city seemed so desolate. We separated when we got into the city with the plan of covering the streets nearby and meeting back up at the station in half an hour. I went back in the direction of the entrance where we came from, hoping to find my sister. There was hardly anybody in the streets and the buildings were all open, so it was pretty easy to get into them. I walked in a few of them thinking that it was fine otherwise why else would the doors be open. There were lots of interesting plants and big holes full of water with animals in them that I had never seen before. I wondered how they had so much water, especially in a desert area like this. I went from building to building and thankfully they were all just one story. It seems the further I dived into the city the more questions I had about this place. Where were all the people? Why were the buildings so small? How did the desert sand stay so strong and firm to use for their buildings? There wasn't a big, tall building anywhere to be seen which was so different. Unfortunately, none of my questions got answered at the time. Just a couple more minutes until I would need to head back to the ship transports. Then I heard a very loud engine-like noise though I knew that it wasn't anything man made. Just then I heard some more scuffles and small screams. Immediately fear came over me, and I made my way back to the ships. As I ran past some of the buildings, I peered into them and noticed that there were more people in them than I had found earlier. I didn't know where they came from, but it must have been obvious that I wasn't very aware of their ways because everyone I saw gave me a frantically concerned look and motioned for me to go inside. I was hesitant, but that wasn't enough to keep me away from them. Two large metal fingers grabbed my shoulders and pushed me towards a building. In a very low monotone voice, "Let's get you inside." Even if I resisted, I don't think I could do much. This Lex was very strong, and his grip was stronger than any other I have ever felt or seen. He must have been through a lot.

"You're not from around here, are you?" asked somebody from inside as we came in. Before I had time to respond another person chimed in,

"Obviously he's not from around here. That screech you heard was a Luucer Piper. Dangerous creatures if they get their claws on ya. Lucky for us though they don't have great eyesight. That's why we built our buildings out of the sand; to blend in. Luucer Pipers have always roamed these lands."

Before he could go on, I blurted out, "My friends are still out there."

"Oh, don't worry about them," he replied calmly, "If they look anything like you other people will have brought them into their homes as well. So, what was your name kid?" He asked me.

"Um."

"Wow, Um. I've never heard that name before," as everybody inside chuckled "Did you forget your name kid?" From behind me a quiet voice that seemed very powerful and controlling forced me to turn around, as everybody else fell silent.

"Leave the kid alone. He's obviously never experienced this before and he's a little nervous being surrounded by a bunch of goons like you guys." His voice was very non-aggressive, and he was definitely someone highly respected, considering everyone listened to him as soon as he opened his mouth. "I am Deraquious, but most people call me Quio for short."

Another person responded, and it sounded like the guy who was asking me questions before, "He's the first dream catcher, kid."

The Trap's Set

In my mind I knew there would be some complications in coming to Aboo to find my sister. Aboo is the dream catcher's city. Most of the people living in Aboo are dream catchers. Dream catchers can be found in all different shapes, races, and sizes just like all dreamers. Typically, however, people don't find dream catchers all that friendly or fun to live around. There is a certain demeanor about them, and they just radiate this; I'm right and your wrong attitude. Sure, you can find dream catchers that are a little bit more normal, but it's not too frequent. All dream catchers have this notion that anybody and everybody who dreams should be shredded to pieces and cease to exist. I don't know how they started or where these random beliefs came from because a lot of dream catchers know dreamers on their home planets. Being a dreamer outside of Ooba is not unheard of. There may be a small number of dreamers on any given planet or region, but there are still dreamers, nonetheless.

It crossed my mind to just sit down and start asking Deraquious all kinds of questions about the dreaming society and maybe by doing so he'd ask me questions about myself, and I could tell him that I was a dreamer myself. How cool would that be to have us two sit down and talk amongst a big group who follow the beliefs of the dream catchers. Good thing that thought was just a thought. A Krimp couldn't freeze time long enough for that thought to even be recognized. I laughed for a second and then thought I was crazy for an idea like that coming into my head.

The moment after Deraquious was introduced to me, it suddenly became so real. Wow, I thought. A real dream catcher right in front of me. It would have been awkward had another not shoved me forward and shouted, "Well, shake his hand why don't ya?" as the awkwardness in the introduction was broken and the room laughed. "Most people tense up in his presence as well boy," the man who pushed me continued to say. "Deraquious, hey." I said with a scratch in my voice. I was terrified that I was around the leader of the dream catchers. I think he was about to ask me my name when a big siren went off and everybody headed out of the room. I was saved by the siren. What name would I have given him had he asked I thought? "Scant maybe," I thought. What a lame name, but it was the best I could have come up with in the stressful moment. Had I told him my name he would have probably done his dream catching techniques on me. Whatever they were. And I would have been history in the blink of an eye. The sirens meant that the Luucer Piper had gone, and it was safe to be outside again.

I quickly made my way back towards the transportation station as that was our designated meet-up point after the thirty minutes of searching in this area of the city. I made it there fairly quickly and I don't think I drew any particular attention to myself. I made it to the station hoping to find the others, but nobody was there. I started wondering, "What if something had happened to them?" I tried to stay calm and look composed as there were other people making their way to the station to catch a ride as well. I had just sat down on a bench when I noticed the pilot coming down the street with another man I didn't recognize. I got excited but stayed seated to wait for them. Everything seemed to be okay with the pilot and the stranger, so I figured he was on our side.

After twenty seconds, coming out of the same street, was Macrill and Tide. Inside I was filled with joy and accomplishment, it took all my energy to not get off my butt and run and hug them both. Yeah, I was relieved to see the pilot too, but not as much as my sister and best friend. The pilot and the new dude came and sat down, right next to me without saying anything. Macrill and Tide finally walked right by us, and Tide put her hand on my knee as she walked by. They entered the ship that had just arrived moments before. The pilot and the fellow with him followed suit. I got up and headed towards the ship. "SKADE!" yelled a voice from down the road. I turned and saw a group of people walking towards the station holding up a hollow device which appeared to have a picture of me on it with a big red caption that was hard to read backwards, it probably said WANTED. I wished it said something else, but the look that they all had in their eyes looked like they were ready to have a change in their lifestyles if they were to get their hands on me and turn me in.

I turned and got on the ship. I pressed a little button above the door signifying that we were ready to go. The group started to yell and run towards the ship. My heart was pounding. It looked like the crowd was yelling some pretty nasty stuff, but I couldn't hear them with the doors closed. I turned and thankfully didn't see anybody but us on the ship. Thankfully these ships ran on their own and it required a lot more credentials and time to stop them from their routes than the people chasing us appeared to have. I hugged Macrill and Tide. I stepped back and hit them both with a barrage of questions, "How did you find her? How are you? Where were you? Where is the rest of your ship's crew? How did you end up here?" Thankfully Tide was with us because she was a little wiser than I was. There are always benefits of having older siblings who are more experienced and have a better perspective.

"What matters is that we are here now, but we have got to figure out how we're going to get out of here," Tide said.

"Oh, you're right". We didn't have time to chit chat. Our ship would come into the main station in about three minutes, and we needed to come up with some plan to get out. We decided it best considering three of us could shift. The pilot, who was a Krimp, wouldn't be able to use his time stopping abilities to be effective and, he'd need to conserve his energy to fly our ship safely. The Krimp with him I found out was on the ship that Tide was on. Only those two had survived without being discovered. His abilities were just as useless as the pilots. Those two would just try and act normal and we'd have to have a quick pace in our step to make it back through security and to our ship.

Shifting always feels weird at the beginning, I turned into the Jubi who was holding the device with my picture on it. My frame was bigger than normal, and my hands felt super different as they always do when shifting into a Jubi. They have the biggest hands. Macrill and Tide also shifted into other Jubi. The ship stopped and the door opened. Nobody seemed to think anything different about us. We just acted normal and headed back towards security. Thankfully it wasn't too long of a walk. We were at the back of a big hold up to get to the tunnel to make it to our ship. The line was moving, but very slowly. At this rate it would take longer than needed to make it out. I looked over at our pilot and we made eye contact. He knew exactly what needed to happen. He and the other Krimp nodded, as if he was aware of what needed to happen as well. We were in line for about 5 minutes when I turned around to glance behind us before the pilot worked his magic and I saw a group of angry-faced Jubi exiting a ship. They immediately looked in our direction, but thankfully they didn't recognize us right away and we were covering the pilot and the other Krimp so they couldn't be seen. Then they seemed to appear motionless. It's time, I thought. We sprinted through the line and made it to the front of the tunnel when our pilot put out his hand. Just as fast as everybody seemed to stop, they resumed as if nothing had happened. Krimps can sense when other Krimps use the time stopping power, but I guess all the Krimps around didn't seem to mind. I think the group following us who were now even further away realized something had happened because they all started to yell and shout while holding up my picture. We quickly went through the doors into the tunnel. There wasn't much security to exit Aboo, but we saw on the other side dozens of security guards helping people enter the doors of the tunnel. We quickened our pace without trying to cause any extra suspicion.

As soon as we left the tunnel, another big siren went off, but it was different from the siren due to the Luucer Piper. The doors to get in and out of the tunnel shut and didn't seem to open as the people from the inside suddenly stopped coming out and the people going into the city couldn't get the doors open. We barely made it out in time. The sirens were still so loud even from the outside. The people who were wanting to go through the tunnel started to become a little uneasy and on edge because of the sirens. Sirens usually bring out some very extreme emotions in people because they know something isn't right. We couldn't risk unshifting until we were safe on our ship so nobody would notice anything. "What's going on?" somebody asked us as we passed them, without responding to them. I could tell the Krimps were a little more tired from using their powers, but they were still able to make it to our ship along with us. We quickly went up the ramp that our pilot keyed to come down as we got there. The pilot immediately went to take off while the rest of us unshifted and crashed on the seats. We were exhausted. Shifting takes a lot out of you, especially when you don't use it too frequently.

I saw my mother very vividly. She was just outside a lasered door. She had cuffs on, with a little jail suit on. Inside the room on the other side of the door was Dakool. He was talking on a device, and the voice on the other side had a familiar tone to it. I was drawn towards Dakool, and he didn't detect me. "The trap is set just like you said," Dakool said.

"Good," Abrack said through the device. "They will walk right into your hands, just keep an eye on the bait." He said and I figured he was referring to my mother who was listening just outside. There was a little scuffle from outside the room. Dakool hung up on Abrack and headed for the door. I wanted to yell out and tell my mom to run, but I couldn't do anything. My view stayed right behind Dakool and to my surprise, when he opened the door and looked for where the noise was coming from, nobody was there. He stayed there for a second, but then went back inside. As soon as he closed the door, I saw my mother behind the door. She looked at me as if she knew I was standing there.

"Don't come." she whispered to me.

I woke up to some turbulence that our ship had hit. "It'll pass," said the pilot. My eyes were extra itchy which usually happens when I shift and then dream. The ripped eyes usually take some time to pass, so it was a good thing we had a long way to go before we made it back to the other dreamers.

"You won't believe the dream I had." Tide suddenly told me when she noticed I was awake. "Mother needs us, we're going back to Jacoby to get her."

"I had a dream too." I responded. "We can't go to Jacoby, there is a trap laid for us."

I guess the pilot couldn't hear our conversation as he yelled out, "We'll be in Jacoby in 3 minutes."

"What?" I said, "We aren't going to Jacoby, it's not safe for us there."

"I know it's not safe, but we need to go get mom otherwise we'll never see her again," Tide said. "Just trust me." I didn't want to trust her, but it seemed I had no choice as I saw the city draw closer. We arrived. I hadn't been back here for a long time, and I had no idea what shape the city would be in. Last time I was here there were riots and killings and lots and lots of chaos. I was a wanted man for doing something that I hadn't done.

We landed our ship in the fields I used to work in. There were people out working in the heat like normal. I guess that was good to see, maybe things did get better, and the city normalized. I don't know if people no longer recognized me, or they didn't care if I was back. When I was accused of killing the Jubi forever ago there was a large group that was on my side and believed I didn't do it. We made our way into the city and some memories of when we first arrived on Ooba came racing into mind. The first time I got off our ship I remember this heat was unbearable. It took months to adjust to the heat and the constant light. Macrill and I would make mischief. My sister went away and then I had a dark phase in my life. I started working alongside my mother. So many memories. At times it was hard to see it in myself, but I felt like I was a more mature grown-up individual than when I was here last.

Tide said we needed to go towards the jailhouse which is where our mother was being held. I don't know if she was thinking we would just be able to walk in there and ask to get my mom out and the guards would let us, but that's how she was acting. I was surprised by the vacancy of the building when we walked in. We had just shifted and probably should have shifted again, but Tide said we would be fine. All this time I was thinking about a trap that was going to be sprung on us as I had seen in my dream just an hour before. We walked straight through the doors and passed a couple of different rooms.

Our mother didn't look too surprised when she saw us, but she was nervous that something was going to happen. I don't know how she would have had time to dream about the future with the guards constantly watching her, but I knew somehow, she knew we would come even while she thought it best that we didn't come. She looked a little skinnier than normal. This was typical as you tended to get less food in the jailhouse. "We have to leave now," she said. I pressed the button just outside her door and it opened up. We embraced for a quick second and then we headed back out the same way we came. I could see as we left the building the people that were looking at us from the windows of the building. For a second, I thought I saw Dakool peering down at us from a window, but as I double checked, there was nobody there. I was freaked out and wanted to start running, but everyone including my mother just seemed so chill about it all. Even Macrill, who was usually the most uptight and on edge guy I knew was so calm about everything. So many questions went through my mind, but my biggest was why everyone in the city was acting so differently. Seeing my mother walk out in a jail suit without any guards would normally be a big red flag. I could tell my mother was getting a little nervous the closer we got to the ship. We had just made it out of the city and I couldn't take it any longer, "What happened here?" I asked my mother. I think she knew what I meant but didn't answer. "I saw you in my dream and it sounded like you knew of a trap, but why did Tide know that we should come get you?" She was still silent.

We made it back to our ship and took off. I was a little confused at what my dream was about, and I felt like my mom knew what I was talking about, but she didn't want to say anything. I decided to put the dream and my concerns out of my mind as we had clearly picked up my mother safely and got out of Jacoby. We now had a long flight ahead of us to make it back to the other Dreamers. We were only 5 minutes in the air when my mother looked me in the eyes and mumbled, "It's a trap."

It Begins

The phrase "Don't freak out" is usually the last thing that people want to hear when they're about to freak out. If you feel like you need to tell someone to not freak out it's probably a good reason to freak out. How else am I supposed to react to bad news calmly and hopefully? Should I say, "Oh, don't worry mother, it's cool" or "oh, I won't freak out I'm super cool and collected when people tell us about a trap that may or may not put all of us at risk?" These are some things that I really wanted to say, and I would argue that most normal people would react or respond the same way I was wanting to. "Why didn't I actually respond in this manner?" I asked myself. But honestly, I don't know. I guess I had a little confidence in my mother and figured that she wouldn't put all of us at risk. She would rather sacrifice herself than put any of her kids in danger.

We asked my mother to elaborate, and this is what we got. She had a dream way back before we were separated the first time and knew that she had to go back to Jacoby. She knew we would come for her to rescue her, but she wouldn't permit it until she went back with Abrack to Jacoby. She was there for quite some time and had a lot of visitors. Abrack, Dakool, even Deraquious came and questioned her. They were all wanting to know where our father was. She would be honest with them and let them know that she didn't know. She really didn't know where he was. She was treated very poorly and not taken care of very well. She went without food and water. She was placed in heat box's, which were these clear boxes out in the open, they are completely exposed to the two stars around Ooba making it hotter inside than outside. Luckily for her, because the heat boxes were so hard to stay alert in; she had some dreams in them. In one of her dreams, she discovered some interesting news. She discovered Abrack was also a dreamer which went against his own laws and that he was seeking to make an alliance with the Clud to eliminate all the people on Ooba that did not follow him. He was in the works of creating thousands of special protective gear for the Clud so that they could withstand the light and heat here on Ooba. She got thinking and wondered how Abrack could work with the Clud as they are wild and act without thought. She then discovered that Abrack knew of a way to get the Clud to work for him. In another dream she discovered that her husband, our father, was still alive and he knew how to heal the Clud. That's why Abrack wanted to know where her husband was because he knew how to heal the Clud, and he probably knew how to control the Clud in some way.

Needless to say, what she told us was a lot to take in. I knew that my father was still alive, but I didn't realize my mother didn't know. She got a little emotional when she talked about him being alive. There was so much information to digest and to think about. "We have to get back to the dreamers and tell them." I said, after hearing my mom tell us of her time in Jacoby.

"Also," my mother said, "We can't go to them directly because we are being followed." She said, "I was the bait and that's why it was so easy for you guys to come free me." It all made sense now as to why there were no guards in the jailhouse when we went to get my mother. "They want us to go to the dreamers which will lead Abrack, Dakool and Deraquoious to them. They have a massive fleet that will be close behind us."

"Well, this complicates things." I thought. "Didn't you say that there would be a way to escape them and at the same time not lead them to the dreamers? " I asked my mother.

She looked down and sighed, "There is."

"And?" I asked "What is it? What's the plan that you had in mind?" Obviously, I thought that we can't lead a whole fleet to the dreamers HQ but at the same time we needed to get their help and tell them of Abrack's dreaming abilities and of his plans with the Clud.

"I have an idea." my mother said, but she looked like she didn't want to do it. She told us she has a tracker chip in her arm that was put in her while she was in the jailhouse. It is connected to a nerve and if we try to take it out it will emit a poison inside of her body that will kill her within days without proper medication. "The other option," she continued, "we might have to amputate part of my arm," trying to sound tough. I knew this was not worth it, if a Gri loses any part of their body then shape shifting basically goes out the window. Shifting doesn't work the same when you're missing an extremity. "There is a herb that can combat the poison." But she would be unconscious for two days while the herb fought the poison. This seemed like the best option, and we decided we'd make that work. This was a tough predicament because the Dream catchers knew of the consequences and didn't think that my mother was capable of cutting her arm off. They also didn't know my mother knew of a remedy for the poison that would be emitted from the chip if we took it out. The only problem was the herb was very rare and only the Mountain Men typically had it. This complicated things, but it was still better than losing part of a limb.

Here was our plan: we would fly back towards the Head Quarters, but we would make sure to go past the mountains where the Mountain Men lived. We would make it look like we were experiencing some difficulties with our ship that needed attention. Upon arrival my mother and I would go and find some medicine from the Mountain Men secretly. I'm sure they haven't forgotten how we escaped them and would love nothing more than to get their hands or paws on us again. After somehow retrieving the medicine, we would cut the chip out of my mom's arm and then somehow get away from a fleet of ships trying to secretly follow us back towards our headquarters. If all went well, miraculously we would all be back at the headquarters with everybody still intact and no poison. We would also be free from all stalkers and then we could relate the news to the dreaming society. It seemed like a simple plan, but things usually didn't go as planned and if they did it was very rare.

Without the tracker in my mother's arm, we would be able to lose the fleet. The ships that were following us must have been trying really hard to stay hidden because not once did we see any ships appear to be following us as we headed towards the mountains near Jacoby. Regardless, we believed my mother that a group of ships were following us.

We were getting close to where we wanted to drop down, so our pilot started to "lose control" of the ship to justify us landing in a place where the dreaming society's headquarters would never be. The supposed ships following us were too far away to see our ship was struggling, but our pilot made it seem like things weren't working properly on our ship and we needed to make a landing.

Leaving the ship seemed unbearable. Even with protective suits it is still so hot. Walking out I saw bushes and small trees all over. I don't know how our pilot even found a spot to land with how dense the plants and trees were, but he did. Based on the smoke that we saw from before we landed, we knew which direction we needed to go to find the Mountain Men. I'm sure we could find the plant that would help protect my mom from the poison, but we knew it would be like looking for a needle in a haystack. Somehow it seemed like a better idea to go closer to the Mountain Men and steal it from them. The Mountain Men always have the herb in their camps because they see it as sacred and believe that it will protect them from evil.

Trying to have a quick pace in our step so the others on the ship wouldn't be waiting too long, we tried to hurry while at the same time keeping our eyes and our ears open for any potential danger. Up in the mountains there were all sorts of creatures and animals that would like to eat us. After wading through the brush for 20 minutes or so we got a glimpse of the backside of a hut. We knew we were just outside of the camp. I'm surprised we didn't hear or see any Mountain Men before we were standing 20 feet behind one of the huts considering how big and loud, they were.

We got nervous for a second, but we knew we needed to get the sacred herb and get out of there. We approached the backside of the hut as quietly as we could. In the distance we heard some Mountain Men chanting. We didn't have any idea as to what they were doing, but we soon realized that all the Mountain Men were gathered near the opposite end of the village. They might have been having a little celebration or ceremony as they are known to do that often. My mother and I took advantage of it and quickly split up and started peering through all the huts and rummaging through the insides looking for the sacred herb. Occasionally, we would look down towards the other end of the village to make sure they didn't notice us. After a couple minutes of looking and losing hope that for whatever reason we wouldn't find a herb, just then I noticed some at the top of a hut. I looked at the other huts and saw all of them had some sitting inside a basket right above the door. Sadly, I couldn't reach it because their door frames are just a little bit bigger than what I was used to. "Get on my shoulders." I whispered to my mother.

"Okay," she said. Trying to keep my balance and hoist my mother up to reach the herb didn't seem too hard, but my mother was just not tall enough to get a good hold of it to bring it down. "Almost have it," she said, as her sweat was dripping all down my face and shoulders. "OVER THERE!" A loud voice said from the other side of the village.

"Hurry mom." I shouted. The Mountain Men started running towards us from 400 feet away. Suddenly it was easier to balance my mom. I looked up and she had it in her hands. I lowered her down and then we both took off for our lives. Having twenty or thirty Mountain Men with angry faces headed in your direction at an alarming speed, considering their size, was no way an invitation to stay there and meet them. Running back through the trees and bushes and getting all cut up and bleeding was way better than seeing what the Mountain Men were about to do to us. Miraculously we went in a straight line back towards the ship without missing a step in our direction. As we approached our ship, we shouted for them to all get in it and to start it up. We could hear the Mountain Men slowly gaining on us. We would normally out-run them, but it may have been our fatigue or some extra power they got from whatever they were doing that caused them to gain on us slowly. We heard the ship start up and get off the ground. We came through the last little bit of trees and bushes and the ship was right there. My mother and I both jumped on and just as we took off a bunch of Mountain Men erupted from the trees behind us. If we had been ten seconds later in leaving, we would have been overrun by the Mountain Men.

I was trying to catch my breath as was my mom. We both looked at each other and smiled. It was good to see my mom again and I remembered just how much she inspired me. She was so strong and resilient. It didn't take long before my mom lifted her arm and grabbed a knife and cut open a little flap of skin that looked like it had been patched up before. Underneath was a little silver chip that was attached to one of the nerves just like she said. She pried at it and tossed it out the window over the mountains. She then started eating the leaves on the herb. Before I could catch my breath completely, she was unconscious. I knew the herb would work and my mother would be able to fight off the poison. After all of that, we knew we wouldn't be tracked by the fleet of dream catchers and started our way back towards the new dreaming society headquarters.

My mother lay motionless on the floor of the ship. She still had a pulse in her arm, but she was unconscious. With everything going on I almost wish I were in her place and didn't have to worry about everything. I felt a big burden on my shoulders sometimes because of the expectations everyone had of me. It would be nice to just disappear for a little while or have people not pay attention to me for an extended period of time. Unfortunately, I don't see that happening anytime soon and I don't think I would be able to live a fulfilling life, even if that did happen. "We're here." Said the pilot from the front of our ship. Somehow our plan to escape the dream catchers' fleet worked, my mother was still alive, and we had made it to our headquarters. It was all a miracle.

I felt so out of place here at the new headquarters. It seemed like there were lots of new faces that I hadn't seen before. There seemed to be almost double the number of dreamers than when we left to find my sister. There were all types of races too, and I wondered how they all got here and what they were doing. "Are there really this many dreamers?" I asked myself as we were walking through the little ravine after exiting our ship. I had never imagined there being this many dreamers.

"Skade!" I heard a familiar voice yell from not too far off. It was Wroff looking right in our direction. He ran towards us and started asking all kinds of questions. "What took you guys so long? How did you find your sister?" "Why is your mom with you guys and why does she look dead? Did you see what's happening around Ooba?" And he probably would have continued to ask another hundred questions had we not stopped him.

"What do you mean about what's happening around Ooba?" I asked him. "This!" he said while raising his hands in all directions towards all the people around us. "The dream catchers, and Dakool and Abrack, have been doubling their efforts to rid Ooba of all dreamers. That's why so many have gathered here. There have been more scuffles all around Ooba and lots of people are starting to rebel against the government and the dream catchers." I guess that made sense as to why there were so many dreamers gathered at the headquarters than before. We were being hunted.

"Follow me," Wroff said, "We have much to talk about."

Our "Successful" Plan

This seemed like a friend reunion. Del, Macrill, Truue, and Tide were all in the room. It was nice to be with everyone again after such a long time. Looking at all of them seemed surreal. I had been through so much with Macrill and Tide. We all came from Zazri when our planet was invaded by the Clud. Macrill is like a brother to both Tide and me. The idea that Tide was dead for the longest time made it more meaningful when we found her again. Meeting Del back in Jacoby in the jail house; he has now become one of my greatest friends. We went through the long mountain range together with limited supplies and faced the Mountain Men. We also faced other creatures that make the Mountain Men run scared. I never would have thought that I would gain a great friend during one of the more difficult parts of my life. Truue, who is technically my cousin; somehow, we made an instant connection as soon as we met. I don't know what it is about him, but he's always there at just the right time he is needed. We'd probably still be running from the Mountain Men had Truue not come and grabbed us in the mountains. He's proved to be very reliable and knowledgeable in many areas. I remember the first time I met him, and I thought there was something off about him. How wrong I was. To think that anything was off or different about Truue makes me feel a little guilty because of how loyal and helpful he is. Not to mention my mother thinks the world of him. I still am confused as to how we're related if we even are, but I guess it wouldn't change any-thing about how I perceived him. The only thing missing was my mother. She was still unconscious and being taken care of with a watchful eye to make sure the poison and the medicine are inter-acting as they should so she can get better. If all goes well, she will be ready to go by tomorrow late in the day.

Wroff was at the head of the table standing with his chair pushed behind him. I still get nervous being around Wroff, not so much because of his physical stature or having a certain look about him, but there's just a powerful presence that he carries himself with. It's kind of hard to explain, but whenever he is with a group of people in any situation it seems as if he is at the head of attention, and everyone seems to have high respect and praise for him. Con-sidering what he's going up against and he's done so far for the dreamers has been nothing short of extraordinary. Without Wroff the dreaming society would not have lasted as long as it has and as a matter of fact it probably wouldn't have even been created. He expects so much from the people around him and inspires every-one to be better. Trying to live up to his expectations requires great effort and can be very daunting, but he'll always recognize any effort to change.

There were a few unfamiliar faces that were sitting around the table as well. One in particular stood out to me. He was a Jubi. Typically, it was rare to see Jubi intertwined with dreamers because it was uncommon. The Jubi have never been known to support dreamers. Probably because the Jubi typically work their lives away and don't have much time for anything else. Then there were other typical Gris, Lexs, and Krimps that were all present. Since we left to go get Tide the numbers have almost doubled. There were lots of dreamers on Ooba that I didn't know about. It only makes sense that some of them were important enough to be gathered together during this meeting that was about to take place. I still wondered what would be discussed and had no idea beforehand as to what we were going to try to accomplish.

"Let us begin," Wroff stated loudly. All the chatter around the room fell quiet in an instant and all eyes and ears were focused on Wroff. The feeling in the room was like one I've never been in before. Thinking about it, it makes sense because I've never been good enough to be in any type of serious meeting and I was still wondering why I was in this one in the first place. I still felt out of place. All the people at the table were extremely impactful people and they had accomplished stuff in their lives. I've just been a little brat most of my life, not even listening to my parents half the time. I hadn't accomplished anything, well at least not anything good. I guess I was accused of murder back in Jacoby, but I don't think that would be a good enough reason to invite me to a meeting like this with other seemingly more important people.

"We need to escape Ooba." Were his next words. This brought a big gasp from the majority of the people, including myself, but some seemed to know this was coming and were completely composed. Leaving the planet entirely just didn't make any sense. Where else would we go that would be safe from the Clud. There wasn't another planet that would protect us from the Clud, that's the only reason we came to Ooba in the first place. Now we were trying to leave, this just didn't make any sense. Wroff continued after the noises around the room simmered down once more. "Only some of us will be leaving, and we need to find Tekrum, your father Skade." He looked right at me when he said my father's name. "We have to bring him back to Ooba." I knew he was alive, and I would be more than excited to see him, but who knows where he could be and would know the type of guy he was. I didn't see it in him to leave other people helpless on other planets when he could offer them help. Here on Ooba, he would have such a boring life and would regret ever coming here to Ooba. There were a lot of questions I had, and I'm sure I know I wasn't the only one with questions swirling through their minds.

"Grab my arm." Wroff said, motioning to all of us to come and put a hand on his arm. All dreamers know what this meant. As dreamers we can all share dreams that we have with others and interpret them.

The scenery looked familiar, and it felt very familiar. We were here on Ooba, and it was still very hot, but there was some shade above us. There wasn't a lot of shade on Ooba because of the two stars orbiting around Ooba, but there was shade this time. I looked up and saw a very familiar looking ship I had seen once before. It was a huge, dark, glossy black with red lines going through parts of the craft. The Clud. I tried looking around to see where everyone else was that I was with in the meeting, but I seemed to be with other random people. I assumed that all the people who touched Wroff were experiencing what I was experiencing. Out of the big ship descended other smaller ships that had their tops exposed so as they got closer to the ground, you could see inside the ship. It was the Clud, and they were equipped with protective gear. They were covered up, so it was hard to see all of their facial features and their big muscles were not as defined under a suit, but they still radiated this darkness. Their red eyes were still visible through the protective suits. They were even scarier than I remembered them being. The Clud erupted from their smaller ships and started running wild through the city. Their screech is not something I would wish anybody to have to hear. It almost makes your head physically shake and you immediately start feeling this weird pain inside your head. Most people just go into shock and freeze up when they hear it. There aren't many people who hear the screech and live, but I guess I was lucky because this is not the second time hearing it in my short lifespan and so maybe I was more accustomed to it compared to others. After a second, I seemed to regain clarity and I could see how damaging it was to those who hadn't ever heard it before. They seemed to lose almost all consciousness and it wasn't that they were confused, but they were just so stunned by the noise that came from the Clud it was shocking. The Clud moved swiftly throughout the city and were taking all lifeforms in front of them without exception. "Whoa," I thought. This was a surprising thing to me. There were even Lex government guards down there along with other Jubi who obviously didn't look like they would be friendly to us dreamers considering their government apparel they had on. The Clud went after all of them. There were none that were spared, and nobody seemed to have mercy from the Clud. As the Clud started getting further and further outside the main body of the city they started coming towards us. I knew it was a dream, but it still felt very real. I could feel my actual body start to get a little more tense and I felt very scared. Who wouldn't be scared when a giant flesh-eating lifeform almost double your size came at you at an alarming speed. There was a group that was about fifty yards out now and getting even closer while still taking down people left and right. I heard screams and yells and people so help-less trying to fight back but to no avail. They were still heading in our direction. One Clud had just taken down a Krimp which didn't have enough power to slow it down to move out of the way, just lost his entire arm. The Krimp was on the ground, dead for sure, and the Clud was on top of him attacking him still. Then it gazed up with part of the Krimp's hand in its mouth and looked right at me. "Uh oh" I thought. He dropped the hand and came barreling towards me. I tried to run and only made it a few yards or so when I felt the Clud slam me from the backside and as soon as I hit the ground I came to.

I was in shock. It was weird still being alive after witnessing something as traumatic as a Clud attacking you, but I knew it was just a dream. I gazed up at the others in the room and saw that others probably had similar experiences when we caught a glimpse of what Wroff was dreaming about. We were all shocked and I think we all knew why.

After having some time to process what we just saw in the dream, Wroff spoke up, "Do you understand now?" Everyone seemed to pause for a second and then one at a time everyone including my-self started nodding our heads in agreement. "The Clud attacked everyone, not just the Dreamers." After that statement we all understood the importance of creating some plan to help prevent the Clud from coming to Ooba. Abrack thinks that he can some-how control and work with the Clud, but he's wrong, the Clud will destroy everyone and everything on this planet. We can't let him use the Clud for his plans because they will fail.

"Let us discuss then," Wroff said, "A plan that will ensure the safety of those on Ooba and possibly the healing of our universe from the Clud." He continued. I knew exactly what he meant when he said healing, he was referring to the idea that my father Tekrum has somehow found a way to heal the Clud. I believe my father is alive, but to think that he can heal the Clud is still an idea too farfetched for me to believe completely.

For the next couple of hours, the meeting would go on while people would take turns talking about different plans that we should pursue. There were ideas from all sides, from the most bizarre and extreme to plain and ordinary. Seeing all the different opinions was very interesting. I could see how the backgrounds of so many people influenced their thinking. People who came from planets with little conflict came up with plans that would involve the least amount of conflict. People who grew up on other planets with lots of violence thought it best to create total chaos and use much violence. Trying to find a plan seemed a little hard with everyone having different opinions. It would have been better if Wroff had already come up with a plan and presented it as the one we were to use, but I guess that's why we were meeting. The biggest challenge that we faced was the fact that we weren't exactly sure what we were getting into. A lot of the details of the plan probably didn't matter much. And there probably was more than one way to go about it all, but not everyone understood that. Yeah, we needed to somehow find my father in a vast universe where he could be on one of hundreds of planets. And to search each planet could take a very long time. Then once we found him, we still wouldn't know exactly how he would help us somehow save Ooba, but also cure the Clud. Yes, cure the Clud. Somehow that was our made-up plan that we had to make happen.

After going at this for hours without gaining any ground or anyone agreeing on a plan someone ran in from outside. "I don't know how, it's too early, but your mother is awake, Skade."

Shaker

This interruption could not have come at a better time. The meeting was getting boring, and everyone began to start doubting the whole idea. Going through with our vision would require great effort and sacrifice. Were we all prepared to give everything for some plan that may not even work? Would it be worth it after all our losses? Was there another easier way that didn't require us fighting against the people who we were trying to save?

Going to find my mother was a much-needed break for everyone. Wroff knew that my mother would provide great insight and maybe help us come up with a better plan that would prove to be successful. She was being watched over in a hut outside of the cave. As I was heading over, I noticed that there seemed to be more people than before. We had only been in the cave for a couple of hours now and it appeared our numbers had already grown. It was a hopeful sight to see so many people gathered together, and they all were on our side. Not all of them were dreamers, but they were on our side, nonetheless.

"Skade." My mother said as she saw me enter the hut. She was still lying down on her bed. Her head was sweating profusely, and her arm was very swollen. She didn't look good at all, but at least she was alive and breathing. She didn't have much strength, as she had just awakened.

"I thought you would be out for longer." Was the first thing I said to her as I put my hand on her shoulder.

"I don't know how, but it seems that my body has interacted with the antidote faster than I had expected."

I wasn't complaining that she was up sooner than expected and, in all honesty, I wasn't all that surprised either. Growing up I remember my mother never got sick and if she ever was sick, ill, or injured she recovered extremely fast. I remember this one story she always told Tide and me growing up, about her fighting off a huge oceanic creature on some planet and she should have died from the fight. She would tell us how she had cuts, scrapes, bruises, and puncture wounds all throughout her body and the next day she said she felt completely fine. There was something about her body that always healed faster than most.

"You won't believe the dream I had." She proceeded to tell me. "Come here." She held up her arm for me to grab. I saw the wound from the chip in her arm. It was so little but could have killed my mother. I put my hand on her arm and waited for the dream to begin.

I began seeing my mother's dream; the scenery was very familiar looking. There were big mountains extending as far as the eye could see. Big tall trees were covering the face of the mountains. The sun was just beginning to go down. It was always pleasant to see what it looked like without any light. Being on Ooba for so long now I almost forgot what it was like to have darkness on a planet. Down in the valley where I was, there were people bundled up for the night. It looked like most of them would not be able to sleep even if they wanted too though. They kept twitching at the smallest noises. There was a wind gust through the trees, and they would all flinch and raise their weapons. They had been in a big fight, and it looked like they were barely hanging on. Some of the men had wounds around their upper body area. It looked like they had scratch marks from claws. If I had to guess, I don't think it would be too far-fetched to say it was from the Clud. There were probably a couple hundred men, but they all looked terrified. It seemed like there was little hope among them to survive any size of attack again. After viewing the scene from an elevated perspective, I was admitted down onto the ground amongst the men. I heard some men talking about how they wouldn't last the night and how they should just give up any hope of rescue by Tekrum. "Whoa," I thought. My father must be here or on his way. I wanted to say to them all that my father would come for them, and he would save them all. I knew my father was always willing to go out of his way to help others, especially in dire circumstances. He wouldn't allow even a disagreement with anyone to prevent him from helping the person if they really needed it. He would go far out of his way to help secure the safety of others.

The screech in the distance was a voice I was becoming all too familiar with in these dreams. "They're coming." shouted a voice from far off. More and more men came out of the little houses armed and were bracing to confront the Clud as they came down the mountains.

"If we hold off this party, we give everyone else on the planet hope." said another voice at the top of his lungs as he was trying to sound confident and hopeful. Parties of Clud were usually smaller groups that traveled separately to try and take down smaller races or populated planets without having to bring in the larger body of the Clud. As scary and powerful as the Clud were, they could still die by different means. The men were ready for the fight even though the moral of the group seemed low.

They came upon us barreling out of the trees so fast. The guns started shooting down towards the direction they were coming from. The Clud didn't go down easily. And it looked like some of them usually endured 3 to 4 rounds before they went down for good. If you didn't get a clean shot at them then it would take even more rounds to bring them down. As advanced as our weapons were, it seemed that the Clud were still too powerful. I saw a group of two Clud jump over one of the houses at the edge of the village and they grabbed the Gri sitting on top of the house as they jumped over. They bit down on the upper half of their bodies and used their claws to penetrate their diaphragm. A couple men started shooting at them from another house next door from the roof and windows. The Clud didn't make it much further. The men were yelling, and you could hear screams in all directions of both the Clud and the Gri. It seemed like the men were holding them off as crazy and unlikely as that seemed. The shooting and screeching and yelling lasted for about 5 minutes. There was a moment when everyone realized the fight was done. The men that were still alive were too shocked to move or stand up right away. I managed to poke my head from above a stack of trunks piled on top of each other and saw a horrific scene. Dead Clud were even uglier looking than when they were alive. Multiple bodies lay with dark red blood oozing from their bodies. Apart from that, seeing nearly a hundred Gri bodies down and bleeding was a sight I won't ever forget. One downside to being a dreamer is having to live with what we see in our dreams.

After a while, the men finally came to and started getting on their feet and surveying the scene before them. Not too long after the men had come down from the rooftops and houses and out from behind the hiding places, there was a big engine noise heard from a distance. It was loud, and it seemed to be very far away. I thought the ship must have been enormous for how loud it sounded, and I couldn't even see it. I glanced around to see the other Gri, and they all seemed to have a hopeful expression on their faces. I figured a ship was coming that wasn't a Clud ship by the way it sounded, but they seemed to believe that the ship was coming to help them. I was hopeful that this was the case. It was so sad to see so many Gri die because of the Clud invasions. Being present during that fight made me even more angry and upset about the Clud and what they were doing to everybody.

The ship was one of the biggest ones I have seen. You could finally see it come out over the mountain top directly behind where the Clud were coming from. It was hard to see still because they didn't have any lights. As they came closer to us there was some type of artillery that shot out of the ship down towards the middle part of the mountain where the Clud had been coming from. There was a large explosion after every shot hit the ground. I didn't think that any Clud would still be alive after those shots. They could survive a lot longer than normal Gri, but the artillery from the ship did some big damage. The ground would shake after impact of the artillery. I didn't know where it was going to land because there wasn't much room. It came and hovered above the little village. It was bigger than the village itself. Suddenly, part of the bottom half of the ship started to descend. The ship didn't need to land. The upper half was still up in the air. As the bottom half of the ship got closer to the tops of the houses, smaller pieces started to separate and descend until they were on the ground. Coming down from the ship were Gri, Lexlands, Rubber Men, and other races that I didn't recognize. The men were so relieved to see them. I didn't know how all these different races had been together on this random planet on a massive ship, but the men seemed happy that they were. The men came out of the ship and started helping the Gri onto the ship and offering them a hand and shoulder to rest on. Entering the descended portion of the ship I realized just how big it was. Yeah, it looked big flying above us, but hopping inside of it made it feel even bigger. When all the men were boarded onto a platform it began to rise. There were even more men inside the lower half of the ship waiting for us with food, bandages, and clothing. I didn't realize it until now, but the planet was cold and the ship inside was much warmer. The men needed to warm up and get some food and rest. After the platform had ascended completely, the lower half of the ship began to rise until it connected with the upper half. This ship could have fit multiple 10 story buildings horizontally inside of it. There were tons of transparent rooms all around the ship where men were doing who knows what inside. It didn't seem like there was much privacy.

I guess everybody knew that I hadn't been through as much as the men because nobody seemed to be helping me. People were crossing in front, to the side, and behind me in attempts to help the Gri who had just been rescued. In all the commotion it was hard to focus on anything in particular. I was just standing there probably with a blank expression on my face. Then from behind me I heard a very familiar voice, "Skade." Before I turned around, I knew who it was that was talking to me.

"Father!" I expressed enthusiastically and hopefully. I turned and saw him standing in between a couple of men. I ran forward to embrace him and he had a smile on his face. Just before I was able to embrace him, I woke up.

There I was with my mother. She was looking right at me. "I know where he is," my mother said. I was so happy to have had that experience. It felt so real, even though I knew it was a dream. That can sometimes be the harsh reality of dreaming, you get glimpses into reality, but you have to wait for things to play out still. Being patient is very hard sometimes when you just want the good things to happen already.

"We have to tell Wroff." I said. Part of the reason why our meetings have been just going in circles was because we didn't even know where we would need to go once we left Ooba. We had no idea where my father was. With this detail figured out all we would need to figure out was a way to get off Ooba and then it would be smooth sailing towards my father.

I helped my mother get out of her bed and we headed towards Wroff. Entering the cave where our meeting was held, before we were interrupted, we saw some of the people still gathered around talking. Some of the people who were in the meeting had left, but Wroff was in there. "We know where my father is." I said firmly as we walked into the room. I put my mother down on a chair knowing that she still needed to rest.

"Where is he?" One of the Krimps I didn't know had asked.

I looked over at my mother, "Shaker, he's on Shaker." My mother replied. There was a gasp in the room, and I was also taken aback a little bit.

"Shaker?" Wroff said. "Are you sure? How do you know this?" He continued to ask. There have been lots of wild stories about Shaker. I don't know how I didn't realize it before in the dream, but it made sense looking back at it now. Shaker was home to some very influential people in the universe. Its planet was very cold and there was always lots of moisture and the visibility on that planet was very minimal due to the storms and the bad weather. The technology and advancements on that planet were second to none. If you ever met anybody from Shaker, you would immediately have a deep respect for them. The people there were very intellectual and wise. Those who lived there usually have been through a lot. The people who lived there endured many things and because of the harsh climate people usually didn't act how they normally would under more friendly conditions. There were usually lots of fights and unrest between people from one city to the next or even within their own cities. The people there knew how to survive.

The Clud haven't been able to take the planet yet because the people were more prepared to fight them off. The men were typically better warriors than other planets. They would be hard to work for and work with on occasion because they seemed to always think they were right. Most of the time they were right, but it didn't make it any easier. If my father was among them this could be a great asset, but also there could be some complications.

There was still unrest in the room and others that were just coming into the room were finding out the news were surprised. I thought it was obvious that we would still need to go to Shaker, but I didn't think that most of the group would agree with it.

After some side talk and chatter had been going on for a couple minutes or so I noticed Wroff thinking deeply by himself about this news. He brought his head up and our eyes met, and he nodded. "It is decided then, we will go to Shaker to find Tekrum." He said firmly and without any stumbling of words or hesitation. His confidence in his decision at first seemed to falter and be lacking, but his stature and body language showed that he was very serious and that's what we needed to do.

"Shaker it is." Said another voice. Everyone else started saying the same thing while raising their hands. "To Shaker." said one, "Shaker." Said another, as all of them expressed that they agreed.

"We're coming father." I said in my head.

My Return to Jacoby

We still didn't know all the details or how everything was going to work out, but we did know we would have to leave Ooba through Jacoby. The Lexlands who worked for the Government on Ooba and provided security were all over, but Jacoby was our best option for multiple reasons. We needed a ship that would be big enough to escape with a group of us while at the same time, not be too difficult to steal. Most ships that were on Ooba were taken possession of by the Lexland officials and they are all very heavily guarded. Jacoby had a ship that was perfect, and it wasn't possessed by the Lexlands according to our intel. Jacoby also had a less concentrated number of enemies or people against us compared to Aboo for example and Bagger. Above Jacoby wasn't a very secure command post like other cities that have more traffic while trying to enter Ooba.

We needed to go out in multiple waves to avoid any serious detection which would bring over extra men to try to stop us from escaping. I know there were plenty of people on Ooba that not only wanted the reward money to catch me, but also some of my comrades. We were deemed as outlaws to society, and we couldn't expect any help from anybody that weren't part of the dreaming society.

The first wave left yesterday. Their primary objective was to go and secure safe houses for all the people who were part of our mission and provide adequate intel on how to get there safely. The second wave, which I was a part of, was to arrive in Jacoby with the least amount of resistance possible. The last wave, which was our biggest wave, would cause a little bit more delay and they would essentially provide cover and create chaos once we had all the necessary details of how we were going to escape Ooba with a small number of those chosen to go find my father.

The day of, we finished up all our necessary preparations. We all had the proper protective gear and enough supplies that we figured we could take with us on our ship. We knew it would probably be around 10 days to make it to Shaker from here. We needed sufficient food and water to provide for everyone on the ship. We didn't know the exact size or details of the ship that we wanted to hijack so we prepared to take lots of food and water and medical supplies. We also had a list of how many people we could take and how many supplies would be needed and were willing to adjust according to the details of the ship that we would have. I was number 1 on the list. If only one person got to go it was going to be me. Wroff wasn't on the list as he knew he would have to stay behind to ensure the safety of the other dreaming society members while we went to get my father. My mother was number six on the list. Macrill was number seven. My sister Tide was number three. We figured she would have an easier time convincing my father to come and help us and my mother would be more useful here on Ooba than my sister would be. My mother wouldn't allow Tide to stay behind while we both left. Number two on the list was Del. I didn't know why Del was so high, but Wroff seemed to have the final say and he considered him to be extremely valuable and resourceful. He trusted that Del would get the job done. Truue was further down on the list so it was unlikely that he would be making the voyage, which was sad. I tried talking to him about it, but he seemed to push it off and did not want to talk about it, which I totally understood. It was just sad to think that one of my good friends, with whom I have been through so much within the last little bit probably wouldn't be coming with me on the trip.

It was time for us to be off. The first wave was there by now and hopefully they had everything set up for us to come. Our wave consisted of fifteen of us. We split up and hopped on three separate ships. We said our goodbyes to everybody else whom we were leaving behind. The rest of our group would be coming in a couple days in the last wave, if all went well. The last wave consisted of a couple hundred people.

We got into our ships and were off. Even though we were about to engage in something that could go wrong at so many levels, our journey seemed so relaxing. There was a peace in the ship that was hard to explain. There would be times throughout the trip where people were just silent and kept to themselves and other times when there would be some group discussions going on about funny experiences. The mood was very light and chill. We all knew what we were getting into and that if anything happened it could be the last time we saw each other, yet there were no bad feelings about what we were set out to do. Deep down inside of me I was a little scared about leaving Ooba. Ooba is a planet that despite all its hardships and the little that it offers, has grown on me. The heat still kills me, and I don't think I will ever get used to it. Always worrying about having a protective suit is not something I will miss. The work isn't too bad and normally the people here are pretty understanding. Most of the people on the planet are refugees like me. Somehow, I am needing to forget that some people turned on me thinking that I would kill one of their family members. I'm still confused about that whole thing, but I know I didn't kill anybody. The government doesn't really do much and they are lazy honestly. The only reason I feel like I've noticed them doing anything at all is because I'm a wanted man now. One good thing about living here on Ooba has been the opportunity to live around so many different people of so many different planets. Some of the Jubi can be hard to live around, but once you get to know them on a little deeper level, they are usually pretty chill.

After the expected time of being in our ship one of the pilots shouted out, "There's Jacoby." We all got up and walked towards the front to see the city. For some reason I was expecting something a little bit more, but Jacoby really wasn't all that special nor all that big or grand.

"Put us down out here," my mother said. "We'll walk in from here."

We were just beyond the fields that I used to work in. There were open fields for as far as the eye could see with some rolling hills. It wouldn't take us too long to walk into the city, but we had to make sure we wouldn't be seen by any Lexlands.

"Alright." I said as we got off the ship, "We're losing daylight, we got to get moving." That comment got everyone laughing a little bit. We didn't care too much about our ship being noticed, so we just decided to leave it there. We grabbed all our supplies and made our way for the city. We had some contact with the first group just before we left our HQ and they said they found a place for us to stay. They were in a building that was deserted near the edge of the city. It seems there were a lot of deserted buildings because of the riots and chaos that had been happening around Ooba. People weren't working their normal jobs and people were moving all over Ooba to find more suitable living conditions around others with similar beliefs. Obviously, the whole city wasn't desolate, but the population was reduced by about 30 percent according to our intel.

After a little bit of walking, we came to an open field full of plants and on the other side was the city of Jacoby. "That's the building." said Wroff as he pointed to one of the bigger-looking buildings. There was a pathway through the plants that we found that looked like it was headed in the direction of the building. We tried to be swift and stay low even though nobody was out in the fields working, which was strange to me. There were always people working in the fields. As we approached the city, we heard some people. We didn't want to look like we were hiding because that would cause suspicion to people who saw us, but we didn't want to get caught either, because I was a wanted man. We were close to the back entrance of the building when we saw two Lex guards in the street. They took a turn and started heading towards the fields where we were. I knew they would know who I was, so my initial instinct was to duck. Everyone else followed suit. There wasn't much room to hide, but we did our best to stay behind some plants that would hopefully make it harder for the guards to see us. The guards came closer and were within 10 feet of us now. Suddenly they turned around and started heading for the street again.

"That was close." I thought. But I spoke too soon. Someone behind me moved against one of the plants and its main limb snapped. The guards still within a small distance heard the snap. They turned around and came straight towards us again.

"Hey!" One of the guards yelled.

"Get them." Wroff shouted as he got up quickly. I got up right after, but the Lexland guards were fast and had already started to make their way towards help. We were just out of reach, and we knew if they made it back for help then our whole plan would be disrupted. Even at full speed they were still out of reach. They were just about to make it past the back corner of the building and be in plain sight of everyone in the streets when there was a loud laser shot. One of the guards dropped dead in his tracks. The other guard was hit, but he managed to keep running. He made it around the corner, and I was an arm's reach away from grabbing him when I was stopped in my tracks. Somebody grabbed me and pulled me back behind the building. It was one of the crew members who had left the group before.

"We can't make a scene out there." He told me.

"But he'll ruin everything, our plan won't work now." I told him.

Wroff then came over, "He's right. We have to let him go, unfortunately. This changes things. We need to act fast." The men who took out the first guard and shot the other guard took us up to our new room while we were in Jacoby.

The room had some burnt walls, and the window was a little charred. There must have been a fire. There wasn't any furniture in the room. Any movement seemed like the floors creaked and it could be heard from everywhere in the building. The one wall that wasn't charred had a big map of Jacoby on it. There was a big red triangle right next to a building at the other edge of the city.

Tide came over and put her finger on the triangle, "That's where the Red Racer is."

"The Red Racer?" I asked.

"It's the nickname for the ship we're going to take to leave Ooba, its actual name is Coronious Raptilious." I had no idea how my sister knew that, but I guess it didn't matter too much.

I turned around and Wroff had just entered. "It is done. They are on their way." I knew he was talking about the rest of the dreamers. They were going to come a little later, but it seemed that we were going to need them much sooner considering the Lex guard got away and was probably now telling the rest of them about us being here. Our plan wasn't going the way we had planned in the slightest, but we still needed to make it work somehow. "They will get here first thing tomorrow and will bring everyone with them." This was a little scary to think that there would be a big fight, all to help a couple of us get away from a planet that was supposed to protect us from the Clud. I questioned multiple times and now more than ever about our plan and our motives behind it all. Would it work out? Would it all be worth it? Would the lives of those lost be avenged or mean anything? Being optimistic about everything or even a few aspects of our plan working out seemed a little tough.

In the meantime, we still had to figure out the rest of the details about how we were going to get out. There we were, sitting in a room back in Jacoby with my mother and sister, Wroff, Macrill, Truue, Del, and some others named Nomree, Billow, and I didn't know the names of the others. There were about 18 of us. A couple of the people that we were with were out on the streets taking in information and watching out for Lexland guards that might be headed our way. We had another place to go to if the Lex did come where we think they wouldn't consider looking for us. We stayed in the same building because of how bad it was, we didn't think that the Lex would think anyone would stay in it because of how bad it was. Due to the fires, it wasn't the strongest structurally and it was probably going to fall over soon. It was a risk staying in it, but we did.

The Red Racer had a large enough fuel tank to give us eleven days' worth of flight. Shaker was about 8 days away, but we might need the extra three days just in case. There was enough room to fit 12 people without any supplies. With all our supplies needed to get to Shaker there would only be room for 10. We also needed to account for my father and probably one of his people coming back with us. So as of now we would have 8 spots open. There was some firepower on the ship, but it was very limited. We couldn't expect to hold our own against even a smaller Clud ship or one of the Lex ships here on or around Ooba. The ship was said to be one of the fastest ships ever assembled. I liked hearing about that. The ship's controls were very simple, and anybody could fly it. There was an auto pilot mode, we didn't know if it was in working condition though.

The ship came from a planet called Armula, carrying eight Gri and four Jubi. It landed eight years ago. It hasn't moved since landing here. The captain of the ship died a few years back, but from the stories we've heard the keys are still in the ship. It was typical all around the universe to leave the keys in the ship because nobody hijacked other people's ships. Ships should still run even without being used for an extended period of time. The door should be unlocked and everything intact. Most ships usually fueled back up to full as they entered Ooba. In the unlikely event that the ship needed fuel then we would have to make a slight detour before leaving Ooba. Fueling ships only takes a couple minutes so it wouldn't slow us down too much, but hopefully it is completely full.

Getting to the ship we were going to go around the outer edge of the city while the rest of the dreamers would be going through the middle trying to draw out most of the guards to them. So many good people were going to sacrifice and put themselves in harm's way while we were going to go around the easier, but longer way to get to the ship. Hopefully the dreaming society would provide enough chaos and distraction for us to get away on the ship. Our exit point from Ooba would have to be straight up from Jacoby as there weren't as many security ships directly above Jacoby.

The ship was also very unprotected. There wasn't a lot of traffic or big groups of people that passed by that way on a regular basis. That part of the city was less popular and not much ever happened that way. The closest building still had people in it, but it was a building full of wanderers. In every city there are buildings that take in people who are just moving in, to help them get settled in before being assigned to live in a building where they will perform their work. The city of Bagger was full of these buildings. That was expected because Bagger took in a large majority of the people who first arrived on Ooba. The main gate to get into Ooba is directly above Bagger. Jacoby, even though it was a smaller city, still had a wanderer building.

There were some footsteps coming up the stairs. I guess that was one benefit of being in an older, damaged building. Nobody could sneak up on us because every movement made so much noise. We all grabbed our weapons and tried to hide the best we could in a small room with not much place to conceal 15 bodies. Macrill was right next to the door peeking out to see who it was coming up the stairs. "All good!" He yelled in a loud voice. "It's one of ours."

The other dreamer who was running up the stairs must have heard Macrill because as soon as he entered the room he shouted, "No," and took a breath, "Not all good, there are a lot of Lexlands and other people not in the government coming this way." This Gri was out on the streets gathering information and keeping an eye on the people as we thought this might happen.

"We have to move now," Wroff said.

Faster than I thought was possible, we cleared the room with all our stuff and headed out the backside of the building. The guards were coming from the center area of the city. We started to go through the backside of the city. "We need to split up and go through the city," I said.

"He's right." Wroff said. We proceeded to go behind the buildings and slowly people started trickling into the crowd as if they were part of the Jacoby community already. The group started dwindling down quickly as behind every building or road that led to the inside of the city more and more of our group integrated into the main crowd. Thankfully, there were lots of people out and about to make it easier to blend in. Blending in was our best chance. If we all stayed together, we would be easier to track. We all knew we had to make it across the city to the new building that we would be staying in. There were still 6 of us including myself and Macrill who hadn't yet gone into the city on the other side of the buildings. Macrill and I left at the next opening. We immediately moved in with the group of people walking through the city streets.

We kept our heads down as much as we could. I was surprised nobody noticed us right away. Hopefully the other four would make their way into the streets to blend in with the crowd. We could hear from a distance some distinct noises coming from a couple blocks away. It was the Lexlands coming to get us. We knew we had to make our way through the city to make it to the building on the other side where we would rendezvous. The crowd started to move a little faster as the Lexlands came closer. They were about two blocks away now and the majority of the people started going into any building to get off the streets. We followed suit and made our way into a building crowded with others. Hopefully the others are safe. There was a large group that passed by, and they all looked like they could do some serious damage. Some of the Lexland guards looked in as they passed our building and I had to be sure to duck behind some others to avoid being seen. After having my head down for a minute, I would poke it back out to see the guards wading through the streets. There must have been hundreds of them, and they were all armed. There weren't any vehicles or low flying ships, everyone was on foot.

I thought it was a little extreme that they would send so many people to find a couple of us, but then again, they didn't know how many of us there were. I would assume that after seeing how many guards passed by there weren't any other guards left in any other part of the city.

It was noisy and very scary looking, but after a few minutes people started leaving the building to go back out. We left with the group and quickened our step to make it to our new hideout before the guards started to head back our way after not being able to find us. We moved quickly and within a half hour we were getting close to where the new hideout was. "There it is," Macrill said as he pointed to a large old, abandoned building.

"Well," I said, "I guess we can only afford to be in the abandoned buildings."

As we entered the building we tried calling out for my mother and Wroff. Nothing. Complete silence. Macrill and I split up and started checking the rooms to see if we could find anyone. Nobody was on the first floor. We made our way up to the second floor and the stairs were just as squeaky as the last building we were in. These Jubi really need to work on creating stairs resistant to the squeaks I thought. We started searching the second floor and still we didn't find anyone. We were about to go up to the third floor when we heard some people come in. We didn't know who it was so we tried to stay as quiet as possible hoping that we could discover who they were before they noticed us. They seemed to do the same thing as us, searching all the rooms. We were standing in a room right next to the top of the stairs on the second floor. After ten minutes we heard some creaking and knew they were headed up the stairs.

"Stay back." It sounded like there were multiple of them, but it was too hard to distinguish how many exactly. They got to the top of the stairs and headed straight into our room. Macrill and I both jumped out ready to fight them when we realized it was Wroff and Del.

"We thought it was the guards," Macrill said. Wroff was a pretty big guy, and I don't think even if Macrill and I both teamed up we could bring him down without any weapons.

"Where are the others?" Del and Wroff both asked us.

"We are the only ones here," I replied. We thought everyone else would have beat us here.

"Well, we'd better keep an eye out to see when the others show up," Wroff said. It's not worth going out into the streets to look for them and we all knew that, so hopefully they all make it here soon.

Del was in the second-floor room where we were hiding, keeping an eye on the street. Every so often he would shout out that someone was coming in. "Two more. Tide and another." And so on he would say. My mother still wasn't back, and it's been over an hour since we first got here. "I see Truue," Del said. I got excited because my mother left with Truue into the crowd so I figured they would be together.

"Is my mother with him?" I shouted from the other room as I came out to go downstairs.

"Nope," he responded.

Truue came in, he had some blood on his protective suit. "What happened?" I asked, "And where's my mother?"

We all knew of the impact and importance my mother had on the success of our mission. Losing her would be devastating for both my sister and I, and our overall plan.

After a second of just standing there staring at the floor, he looked up and we connected our eyes, "Your mother was taken."

Help Arrives

This is the second time that this has happened. My mother had a knack for being taken by the enemy. Sometimes I wondered how she was so unlucky, but I knew if there was a choice between her and anyone else, she would rather herself to be taken. When we asked Truue about it all he told us was; "one moment they were together and the next they weren't together." He continued by saying, "As I looked through the crowd to find her, thinking she would still be close to me, she was being taken by 4 guards." Their path that they took was closer to the guards than the one we took. "There were guards all over and we didn't have time to hide or escape them, so we just tried blending in, but they found your mother."

I wanted to go out and find her and bring her back, but I knew better. Odds are she would probably be surrounded by lots of guards. Dakool, Deraquious and probably Abrack were all interrogating her right now. My mother knew too much for her not to have a high priority on her head compared to other jail house members.

I was sitting down in the corner trying to keep my emotions together and stay hopeful about our mission. Right now, more than ever I felt like we had no chance and everything we were doing wouldn't work or be worth the sacrifices or losses anyway. The thought crossed my mind to just leave quietly and run away from everything and everyone. I knew I couldn't do this. After sitting there for some time Wroff came over and sat down next to me.

"I know how you feel." Was what he first said to me. "I too have lost family members and close ones." I looked at him and knew he had been through a lot. He was a great man and that's why he's been trying to fight back against injustice. He had his eyes locked in on mine, "The dreamers will be here in 2 hours, we'll get your mother back. Don't worry." He sounded so confident and that was reassuring to me. "Come on, we've got some planning to do."

We all gathered together on the second floor where we had set up our intel just like the last building we were in. The map of Jacoby was now laying on top of a table this time. Some of the people were out keeping an eye on things in the city so we wouldn't be surprised by anything like last time. This would probably be the last time we all got together in a very long time or ever depending on what happens in the next 24 hours.

Jacoby was separated into quadrants J3-J17. I don't know why it didn't just start with 1, but I guess it didn't matter. My mother and I lived in J14. Currently we are in J4. The Red Racer was very close to us in J5. We estimated that it would take about twenty minutes on foot to make it to the Red Racer from our current location. It could be delayed depending on the fights that we were expecting to break out. There were about 1800 guards here in Jacoby. Once word got out about what was happening in Jacoby help would come, and it would first come from Eckles. Eckles was a smaller city that only had 200 guards and it would take them a little over an hour to get here.

Our intel confirmed that there were only 14,000 people in Jacoby. Lots of them would stay out of the fighting and hide in their homes, while a quarter or so we were hoping would join us and we figured a quarter of the rest would join the government. We had a couple hundred dreamers coming to create some distraction for us to escape. We would tell the dreamers that were going to arrive in a little under an hour about where they were supposed to go and hope that they could create enough commotion for us to leave safely.

We would have the dreamers split up into groups of 30 or so and they would go into different quadrants creating chaos. The sad part about our plan would be the fear that would be instilled into the people who lived in Jacoby who weren't on either side. Hopefully nobody would get hurt that didn't need to be. We were hoping that as soon as the dreamers started creating chaos the people would either go inside their homes or closest buildings and those that were with us would join and those that would be against us would obviously make it known by fighting against us.

We would have people initially attack every quadrant except J3, J15 and J5. We relayed this information to Dreamers on the way and told them to use whatever means necessary. Some of them would stay in their ships to have some air support while others would go on foot and use all types of weapons to create enough chaos to keep the guards occupied. I wondered why we couldn't just go and take the ship without causing a bunch of chaos, but I realized if the guards weren't occupied with a more present danger caused by the chaos, they would send multiple ships after our ship knowing that people need permission to leave Ooba through Jacoby. We could probably outrun them, but we didn't want to risk that so we figured it would give us the best chance of success by creating chaos for the guards to be preoccupied with more immediate problems.

The time had come, and we got the call. The dreamers had arrived in Jacoby. They were all in their proper quadrants throughout Jacoby. They were told to start the attack at the hour mark, which was in 2 minutes. Our room was quiet, and we were all left to really think about what was about to happen. The dreamers were told not to cause any damage to any innocent citizen, but if anyone raised up arms against them, they were told to attack. It was hard to believe that nobody that didn't need to get hurt wouldn't actually get hurt. I knew accidents would happen and people would make mistakes or misfire. The reality that everyone here in Jacoby would be affected in one way or another was sad. There are so many good people who are just completely oblivious to the corruption of the government and its leaders here on Ooba.

Abrack, even behind the scenes, is still heavily influencing all the government's decisions here on Ooba. He is putting lies into everyone that he meets. All the government just doesn't like dreamers because Abrack told them not to like us. I guess it didn't matter anyway, I knew they were not going to change so that's why we need my father to help save us from the Clud when Abrack figures out a way to bring all of them here safely.

BOP. There was an explosion of gunfire hitting the buildings. It has begun. Within a couple of seconds there seemed to be large explosions coming from all directions from the start of the attack. Zu zu. There was immediate gunfire right outside our building as people were using their laser guns. We heard lots of screaming and there were moments when it seemed like the time would be paused. We knew the Krimps on both sides would be using their powers to make a difference. Thankfully we had some Krimps on our side so we wouldn't lose any time. The Jubi that were fighting were probably creating as many weapons and shields as they could without passing out from using their powers. The bad thing about shapeshifting in this situation is that it wouldn't help at all. People would return fire if we fired at them and vice versa. We wouldn't want anyone on our side to shoot at us as we were shifted anyway. Also, shifting requires the most energy and we couldn't do it for a sufficient period without falling asleep after.

We needed to act fast. If somehow our dreamers would hold back the larger force, they would only have an hour before fresh new Lexland guards would come to help. This was being optimistic. We all had our stuff packed and we made our way down to the first floor to go out towards the Red Racer. On the first floor there were dreamers hiding out shooting from the inside at some Lexlands across the street. The noise was so loud it sounded like a giant Clud ship was 100 feet above us. We had to yell at the dreamers to give us cover fire as we needed to leave towards our escape ship. There were Lexlands on all sides of us firing in different directions. The dreamers had split up in the quadrants and were raining down fire on all sides. The surprise seemed to be working right now, but we didn't want to wait around long enough for their forces to regroup and make more effective advances on us.

The dreamers in the building split up and started shooting in both directions providing a little path for us to head to the building right in front of us. We all had guns and were shooting them as we ran to the building in front of ours. "We're going to be under heavy fire the whole time" Wroff shouted. It was hard to hear it, but thankfully I was an expert lip reader. There was a group of Lexlands and Jubi standing on the corner behind some big walls that I'm guessing the Jubi created because they didn't look like they were normally there. I started firing in that direction. Out of the corner of my eye I saw a couple men drop from the group that gave us the initial cover to make it to this building. I turned and saw the backside of my Tide and Macrill firing towards another group some 80 feet away. We had to stay low as people were firing upon us. We seemed way outnumbered, but we were putting up a good fight. I saw people who were running into the buildings unarmed knowing that they were neutral in the fight. I heard from a distance, other ships shooting into buildings. The noise from the glass shattering against the ground was faint, but distinguishable. We started to move along the front towards the side of the building. We stopped on the corner and saw some others fighting in the street. There were bodies on the ground with obvious laser wounds in them. So many had already died. We needed to complete our mission otherwise all these deaths would be for nothing. People were shot and still fighting.

"Go!" I told Tide as I pushed her and Wroff forward to cross the street while the rest of us gave some cover fire. I quickly followed right behind them as I shot down the left side of the street. Macrill and Tide were shooting off to the right. We quickly went to the front of the building and hid behind some big pillars.

"We need to keep moving" I yelled at our group hoping they would understand me even if they couldn't actually hear me.

While we were facing our own struggles to make it to the Red Racer, all over Jacoby our forces were dwindling swiftly, but they were still fighting. We all knew that this could very well cost us our lives if we were to go through with our plans. Over in J8 was the worst of it. J8 was where the Lexland guards had their security building, and the jail house was also in that quadrant. The Lexland guards had made it back to their building when all the attacking began. The group that was sent there was heavily outnumbered by the guards. There were only a handful left and they wouldn't last much longer than 10 minutes. There were dreamers' bodies all around on the streets and in the buildings. They got little help from the citizens in that area due to the amount of loyal Abrack followers in that area. There were some that had been taken captive and they would be questioned and executed eventually. Over in J16 on the edge of the city the men were having some success. There were few guards out in that area, and lots of citizens had joined in with the dreamers. It seemed like the guards there were waiting for reinforcements to come to help bring down our forces. In J11, flying through the air was a ship that was fully armed and raining down fire on the streets and buildings. In that quadrant all the streets were cleared up. The ship's firepower was doing serious damage, and it would take a lot more than a simple guard's laser to take it down. Most of the guards in that area made feeble attempts to slow down the ship but to no avail. There was constant laser and blasters being fired in all directions all around Jacoby. Our dreamers could not have done a better job considering the circumstances and our numbers.

We quickly went from building to building, occasionally stopping for cover. Sometimes we would turn the corner and run into a group firing directly at us and we would have to go around the other way. Sometimes we would go into the building and go up towards a higher floor and break the glass in an open room and shoot down on the men below. The citizen buildings that we entered were mostly in their rooms and so we didn't need to maneuver around any of them while we were in the buildings. There were some ships that were manned by the government that flew over us a couple times and we had to make sure we were inside the buildings when that happened. We didn't stand much of a chance going up against the ship's firepower. We had to run and jump over bodies lying on the streets and right outside of buildings. The number of people dying during this whole process was a number

I didn't want to know. I knew by this point more than half the dreamers were probably taken captives or they were lying on the streets dead. This was the harsh reality of our plan. I couldn't think about it because I knew I wouldn't be able to function with all of that on my mind while trying to stay clear of the guards shooting in our direction.

We had just passed through to quadrant J5. Somehow, we were all still alive. A couple of us didn't look so good with all the rubble and dust all over us. Some of us had some scrapes and scratches from glass shards and ground burns. About 2 blocks away was the Red Racer. We continued pressing forward with there being less support in this quadrant from the dreamers. Because of this there were also less guards, which made it nice. Almost anything was better than having enemies all around you trying to shoot at you. Peeking around a corner knowing that you may not be able to bring your head back was terrifying. We were heavily out-numbered, but somehow, we had managed to make it this far. We slowly went from building to building hoping not to encounter any serious problems.

We still had some communication with the other dreamers from around the city and checked in on them throughout the whole time. People were falling all over to the government and the dream catchers. The dream catchers that were in the city already only tried to stun the dreamers because they always wanted to bring them in alive. Getting captured by a dream catcher usually meant extensive questioning and maltreatment in many forms. People who got caught rarely got away, and most who did were never the same. Thankfully Jacoby didn't hold as many dream catchers as did Aboo. Our forces were about depleted when the Red Racer came into view. "There it is!" I shouted at the top of my lungs. It was on the edge of the building on the outside of the city. We ran forward.

There were some people on our left firing at us when Tide yelled, "I'll fight them off, get to the ship." Another Gri from our group stayed with her as the rest of us ran towards the ship.

The ship was older and had probably been here for the past 15 years. Despite it not being used it seemed to be clean. The ship was bigger than I had imagined it, but we still had a lot of supplies that we needed to load into it. On the backside of the ship was a darker red panel. That was the key into the ship. I quickly pressed my hand onto it and the back third of the ship separated itself. A long ramp then descended from under the ship, and it attached itself to where the ship had just been separated. As we started to load up the supplies onto the ship, Macrill went and turned the ship on to make sure it all was working okay and that it was fueled. "Everything's good," Macrill shouted from the front of the ship.

As we finished packing up all our supplies Tide came running back towards us shouting, "They're coming." I didn't know who she was talking about at first, but right behind her was a very large group of men that didn't look like they were on our side.

We were all gathered around the ship with our guns aimed at the approaching crowd. Macrill stayed on the ship. I knew that with our current circumstances, Macrill, Tide, Del, and I would be the only ones leaving on the Red Racer. Just then it occurred to me that we were missing Truue. He must have fallen behind somehow, but I didn't know when. "You guys need to go now." Wroff shouted.

Before I could respond I noticed something in the approaching crowd which consisted of some dream catchers and guards. I saw in the middle of the group some people carrying someone. They stopped 20 yards in front of us. They also had their weapons, but they were not firing at us. Then the body that was being carried was brought forward. "Mom." I shouted, but I knew I couldn't get her without being taken myself. She looked very bad. She somehow managed to tilt her head up and I could see her face was badly bruised and bleeding.

"Go!" she mouthed. I was motionless. I didn't know how this could happen to my mother. I was so heartbroken. Tide tried to run up to her, but Wroff grabbed her and told her to get into the ship.

After my mother had appeared, Abrack, Deraquious, and Dakool all emerged and walked a little closer to us. "Skade," Abrack said in his cool deep voice. "We know all about your little plan." He then pointed behind him and out came Truue. He had a little smirk on his face.

I don't know how any of us didn't notice before, but he somehow disappeared on our way to the Red Racer. He's the one that was with my mother when we left our last hideout, he led the dream catchers directly to them. "Traitor!" I yelled out. My emotions seemed to come back really quick. Anger and frustration seemed to fill every fiber in my body. "How could you do this to us? Why'd you do it?" I shouted at Truue. "We trusted you." I continued, "My mother trusted you."

He just had a little smirk on his face, but he kept his mouth shut. I raised my gun in his direction, but before I could get a shot off Dakool put a blade up to my mother. I held the gun up and I was so angry, but I knew I couldn't do anything that would cause my mother's death. After a minute I lowered the gun down. "Good," Abrack said. "Why don't you guys come away from the ship and turn yourselves over and we'll be sure that everyone gets a fair trial and treatment?" Abrack continued to say. We all knew a fair treatment was just words coming out of his mouth and in all reality we would all be executed. Wroff was still behind me, and he tugged at my shirt motioning for me to get into the ship.

Abrack seemed to know what was happening, "If you guys leave in that ship you won't make it out of Ooba and everyone who doesn't get in the ship will die" Abrack said. "We have extra ships above the exit path of Jacoby," he continued. "We know about everything." It made sense considering Truue has been with us the entire time, he has been feeding them information about all our plans and whereabouts.

We were at a standstill. I don't know why they didn't just rush us, but as I started looking around, I saw people looking at us from the inside of the building in front of us. People were watching how Abrack and Dakool would handle the situation. I realized they still needed to have their trust, so they tried to be diplomatic in their approach to appeal to the citizens watching. Abrack was a smart yet cunning man.

Wroff seemed to have had enough of the debate as he grabbed my shirt and yanked me back. I went flying onto the bottom steps of the ship. "Tide and Del go, Macrill take off." Wroff shouted. The men started to rush towards us, and I didn't have much of a choice. Tide and Del came and picked me up and we all sprinted up the stairs. As soon as we got up onto the ship the stairs came back in, and the ship closed itself.

"Hold on," Macrill shouted from the front. If we did somehow make it off Ooba, Macrill would not be the one driving on our journey. We all got thrown against the deck from the speed and lack of driving finesse that Macrill took off with. After getting to my feet, I went and strapped myself into the other seat next to Macrill. "Our defenses better work, because we're going to need them getting out of here." Macrill said to me. We saw lasers flying past us and we felt some hit us from the men below, but they didn't do much damage. "Our defenses seem to be intact." Macrill said. I tried to look down to see what was happening to Wroff and the others we left behind, but I couldn't get a good angle from where I was seated.

We made a beeline straight up towards space. I saw a couple other ships that started to come in our direction, but they couldn't keep up with our speed and we slowly increased the gap between us and them. "If Abrack is right," I started to say, "There will be more ships up there."

"As old as the Red Racer is," Macrill said, "I'll still take it over any ship from the government."

"Let's hope you're right," I said.

Speechless

From what I remembered, entering Ooba for the first time wasn't very complicated, in fact it was easy. I guess leaving was a little more difficult for people, or maybe it was just us. I didn't know why it would be hard to leave Ooba because nobody wanted to leave. Outside of Ooba laid problems way worse than things you would encounter on Ooba. With the direction and path the universe was heading, anything outside of Ooba was probably worse than most anything on Ooba. Ever since the Clud did the little thing of transforming into flesh eating creatures the universe has been a little different. There used to be a lot of interstellar travel and friendly trading relationships from one planet to another. We used to travel outside our world all the time without fear of anything ever happening to us. We could travel all over Zazri without getting into any trouble for being from a different city. Outside people always came to Zazri for a variety of reasons. The Gri on Zazri can sometimes be a little hard on each other, but when it comes to outsiders, we were some of the most friendly Gri you could find in the universe. Race wasn't a big deal back in the day. One Lex could intermingle, socialize, and do businesses with any Krimp, Rubber Men or even Gri without any problems. My father worked with a lot of Jubi in his days who helped him build lots of useful and practical things to facilitate life for others. There were very few wars on any planet. There were even fewer wars between one planet and the next. Now, when we would meet somebody who had just recently arrived on Ooba, we would ask them about the outside and it was usually never pleasing to hear. Races became corrupt and violent. People were harder to work with and it was hard to trust anyone. Some people, believe it or not, are super happy with the Clud and what they've done. The Clud race has opened the eyes of many that violence and lack of discipline can help you survive over one another. People who look at the Clud and think "They're doing it right" are just sick in the head. Nothing about what the Clud have done is respectable or honorable. They are a violent race running unchecked around the universe going from planet to planet destroying anyone and anything in their path.

Anyway, we quickly sighted some ships above us as we approached the outer edge of the planet and knew we were in for a fun time. There was a big open circular station that we had to pass through. Ships that don't go through the hole get shot down from what we've heard. Every ship that goes in and I guess out, that were not from Ooba need to go through a station. Going through the station was customary, and it's where there was a brief security check. When you finished coming through the station, they would tell you in what city you should stay while on Ooba. It was more of a suggestion, but if you did go to the city, they told you things usually worked out better.

There were quite a few stations around Ooba, and they were all well above the ground. Above the bigger cities were usually the bigger stations and there were smaller stations above smaller cities. Jacoby was one of the smaller stations compared to some of the other ones. The other stations were heavily protected and secured compared to this one, but unluckily for us it seemed they knew we were coming so they had more ships and guns placed to stop us from leaving.

We could start to see the stations without any form of magnifying device. There were multiple ships circling the stations. We were outnumbered 10 to 1. Our odds were not looking good from a number's standpoint. The ships must have seen us coming because 4 of them went to cover the exit point and the other 6 ships started their descent to meet us. I thought maybe we could talk it over through our intercoms to let us through, but I soon knew it wouldn't work. "Here they come," I said. Tide and Del both strapped in and braced themselves. Macrill pushed on the communication button that allows us to talk to other ships in the area.

"So, y'all going to let us through or are y'all going to let us through?" He said confidently as if they would be dumb not to let us through. I don't know how he could be so composed under a situation like this but then again Macrill was weird like that sometimes.

This was the first time I think any of us had been in an air fight on ships. They descended faster than I thought. The first one started firing at us. Luckily, they had bad aim, or maybe they were just giving us warning shots. I'd like to think that they just had bad aim. Even from a distance I could tell their ships had up to date technology. Our ship was, relatively speaking, in great condition but that's because it hasn't been used very much.

"They have nice ships." Del shouted from the back, "But they're bad pilots."

"What makes you say that?" I shouted back.

"Do you think they get much practice?" he then asked me.

I thought about it for a second, "Yeah, you're probably right. I guess that makes sense for their terrible aim and why they have 4 ships just sitting by the exit. They're just trying to get in the way so we can't pass."

"Let me know when you need me to come take the handles." Del then shouted at us again. I didn't know exactly what he was talking about. I'm trying to recall our time together since we met in the jailhouse, but I never heard him mention anything about being a great pilot.

"All good." Macrill said. I was going to have him come up, but I knew Macrill wouldn't want that now that he said all good. I've been on the ship long enough with Macrill at the wheel and I know you can't get much worse than his driving abilities.

Macrill took a hard left turn to avoid some gunfire coming down towards our right. We stayed on that path while two ships pulled up behind us. We did some basic maneuvers to avoid being hit by their weapons. Our ship started to really shake as we made more and more quick turns, barrel rolls, and spins, as we evaded the oncoming ships and their weapons. My body felt like I was just thrown into a circus that was never going to end. We pulled up normal for half a second and then we were back making spins, twists, and rolls again. One moment we would be upside down with a ship right below us and the next we'd put on the brakes and shoot upwards and have 3 other ships right in front of us.

Escaping these ships and exiting Ooba seemed impossible. Considering how we had made it this far and to come up so short would be the worst thing that could happen. We had to make it out now after going through everything. This went on for about 10 minutes trying to evade and at the same time shoot down the other ships. If they would just let us through, we wouldn't worry about shooting them down, but they chose not to listen.

BOP

We heard a big thump sound and immediately loud sirens went off in our ship. "PROTECTIVE SHIELDS DOWN" It repeated 3 times then went quiet. We all got jerked forward as one of the many missiles hit us from one of the enemy ships. "This is not good." Macrill said. I could tell he tensed up a little more and was trying extra hard to avoid being hit again. Our little ship was designed for speed and long-distance traveling, not for resisting other ships' firepower. With our defenses down I didn't know how much longer Macrill would be able to avoid their ship's weapons. They were trying to take us down considering how much they were firing at us. If they wanted us alive, I think they would have tried another plan.

We were heading far away from the exit with 3 ships on our tail. We were increasing the distance between us when Del unbuckled his seatbelt. He walked up to Macrill and put his hand on his shoulder, "I'll take it." I think this hurt Macrill's pride a little bit, but he still got out and let Del take command of the ship. I still didn't know that Del was a pilot, but he made it seem like he could get us out of our situation.

We made a quick turnaround and went head on in the direction of the other ships were coming. He slowed down and then, when we got within a couple hundred yards, he shot a missile that I could have seen coming and maneuvered out of the way. "We let this guy take over?" Was the initial thought after his misfire. The ship easily maneuvered to the right moving closer to the other two ships. He quickly cranked up the speed of the Red Racer and made a quick adjustment to head straight at them from a different angle. He then fired a missile directly at the ship in front. The ship was completely obliterated and due to the explosion, its ship's parts flew back into the other two ships. The two ships took a lot of damage and immediately started descending towards Ooba. There was black smoke emitting out of both the ships. "Whoa" I said out loud, but it was soft enough that he couldn't hear me. I guess I could have been wrong about Del. I was a little curious now about his flying background. I was suddenly feeling more confident in our chances of success and my only question was, why didn't we give him the controls of the ship sooner?

We started our way back towards the exit station knowing that the other few ships there wouldn't be able to stop us from leaving. We were a minute or two away from a successful exit of Ooba. We started to get close enough to see the other 3 ships that were there. I don't know what happened to the fourth ship, but I wasn't complaining that there were less. A little further away from the station were some black dots that slowly got bigger as we got closer. "That can't be, can it?" I asked, pointing in the direction of the objects coming towards us. We then heard through our transmission a familiar voice. "Hope you guys didn't think it would be that easy." And we all knew the voice. It was Truue. I wanted to scream at him, but I knew they couldn't hear us. When we were hit, our outbound communication was also taken down. Only being able to hear Truue, but not being able to respond to him was terrible. I thought I was going to lose my mind. I wanted nothing more than to yell at him.

Truue continued, "We have 8 other ships with us. You are heavily outnumbered, and we have everyone down below surrounded.

The only way they'll live is if you guys turn yourselves in." Then there was a pause. I think he was expecting us to respond, but we couldn't. I guess that gave me a little satisfaction knowing that he was expecting us to say something, but we didn't. He didn't know that we couldn't because our communication systems weren't a hundred percent. "They're all going to die if you don't comply." Silence.

"They won't kill them," Del said. "They'll be used as collateral for the Clud, and Wroff and your mother are both bargaining chips that they won't just get rid of because of who they are." That made sense, but I guess I didn't process that which was a testament of my youth still. Going through what I have to go through is not normal for anyone my age. It's a good thing I have lots of older people who have more experience than I do to get advice and guidance from.

We proceeded towards the exit point. Their ships split up to try and take us down from multiple angles. We headed straight towards the main body. Truue was in the front ship, and he seemed to be leading the other ships. The ships were the same model as the other ships we had taken down and evaded. "Hold on." Del said. He revved up the speed real quick and we went straight towards the oncoming ships, then he did a quick nose drop right before we would make impact with the ships. We immediately went under them and the ships from that point on started firing at us. We weaved in and out going left to right while still trying to head towards the exit point of Ooba. I don't know how we didn't get hit with all the firepower the 8 ships combined had, but I'm glad Del was now at the helm instead of Macrill. Even with all the spinning and rolls that we were doing I could still see the weapons being fired fly right by us. Somehow none of them hit us.

Because we were faster than they were we were creating distance between them. We were coming up to the exit point and we would have to quickly maneuver around the ships there to fly out of Ooba in one piece. The 3 ships that were guarding the entrance got out of position and started to head towards us while firing upon us. Del purposefully waited a couple times to move at the last minute before we were hit knowing that the other ships were behind us. Some friendly fire took down two of their ships. The men here on Ooba were not that experienced with ship fighting and their reaction and anticipating speed was subpar. There were now 9 ships firing at us trying to take us down. We were now right below the exit where lots of other guns were stationed and firing upon us. We would make one move and free ourselves from the range of 2 or 3 ships only to find ourselves in the line of fire of another couple ships. Making a break for the exit a couple times but having to quickly avert our path due to ships or weapons. It seemed like we were going in circles forever and not having any real progress. Surviving was all we were currently doing. We weren't going anywhere, but at the same time the other ships weren't hitting us.

The only thing we had going for us were our weapons. As soon as Del realized we couldn't escape with all these ships and stationed guns firing at us, he started to fire back. Saving our weapons for when we were off Ooba was a high priority because we didn't know what was out there. Up to this point we had only fired a couple of missiles and they were all effective. The ship didn't carry many weapons because they usually slowed it down. The upside to firing our weapons, we would get rid of some weight, and we could go faster. Del didn't bother firing at any of the stationed guns because those weapons were easier to avoid. Firing the weapons towards the other ships was our best option. Hopefully we don't use them all to get off of Ooba, but if we did then we would have to make do without them.

Del continued to sway left and right avoiding gunfire while at the same time trying to fire at the other ships. One ship was close on our tail, and it was hard to shake off, but it seemed Del wasn't trying to shake him off. He slowed down, allowing the ship directly behind us to fire a missile at point blank, but Del timed it perfectly as he immediately turned the engines off and the ship dropped. The missile went right over our ship and went straight at another ship and blew its bottom half open. They started hurling down towards the ground. Once again friendly fire was used to our benefit.

It almost seemed as if every time one of the ships went down, we could hear Truue yelling into his mic geared towards the other ships. He was not happy. I was totally okay with him not being happy. It was still very emotional hearing his voice though. We had been through so much. He had saved us on many accounts and proved to be loyal on many different occasions, yet in the end he chose to side with the enemy. I don't think I could feel any sympathy for him if he were to get shot down by us or if something terrible were to happen to him. I know he was a great driver of other vehicles, but it didn't appear that he was the best pilot of his ship. He didn't seem to do much. Every time we flew around him, he seemed to be two steps behind Del. I was very stressed during the whole thing; however, Del did have this calm presence about him that gave me more hope that we would make it in the end.

A couple times we flew close to the exit station on our way out with no other ships in our way to stop us when the stationed guns would fire an extra number of shots toward us, and we would have to deter our course. The weapons on the station weren't the best, but we couldn't take any more damage and there were a lot of them. Risking it was not an option for us at this point. Right now, I was thinking how nice it would have been to have another Jubi with us to help fix our ships shields, but we didn't and that was that. Del seemed to be managing well without the shields anyways. He was even more focused because he knew there could be no mistakes. He didn't say much during the whole fight. He was dialed in. Occasionally I would look back at Macrill and Tide who were both looking nervous. They were both holding onto their seats as if letting go would lead to their immediate death.

Del continued to evade and take down the ships one by one. There were still a handful of ships remaining, but it was easier to manage as more and more of them got shot down or collided with another ship and went down. Truue was still flying, but he wasn't much of a threat. With less ships firing at us, Del could think clearly. "I know how we're going to evade the stationed guns, but you're not going to like it," Del shouted out while looking directly at me. "Over on the outside edge of the entry exit station is where the maintenance workers drop off to go check on all the structures and weapons to make sure they're good. The guns can be overridden, and we can shut them down long enough for us to fly through the station. You'll have five minutes to go and shut down as many guns as you can. We can evade and keep the other ships busy while you take down the guns."

"How am I supposed to shut off the guns?" I asked.

"There should be a switch behind all of them that will reset them. They will shut down for five minutes and then they will turn back on."

"Well, this came out of nowhere." I thought. I thought to myself why I had to be the one to go, but I would rather do it than put my sister and Macrill into that situation. I didn't trust myself any more than them, but I wouldn't be able to live with myself if anything were to happen to them. "Okay," I said, "Drop me off."

Del evaded two incoming missiles and turned on the speed towards the drop off point. We outflew the other ships and arrived at the spot where I would hop off. "Remember, five minutes is all," he told me. The bottom half of the ship separated, and the ramp was let down. I quickly unbuckled myself and ran towards the back. I looked at Macrill and Tide briefly then headed down to the station.

"Be safe." Tide shouted as I ran down the ramp. It felt nice being on solid ground. Well, more solid than some ship flying through the air. Technically speaking I wasn't on solid ground at all, but it still beat being in the tiny ship strapped down with other ships trying to shoot you down. As soon as I was off, Del recapped the Red Racer and took off while three ships were heading in their direction. I ran off down the station hoping that they would be okay. I spotted the first station gun that wasn't shooting because the Red Racer wasn't in the area. It was a way's away, so I had to hurry. It was on the edge of the opening of the station. There was a ladder that took me down to the same level as all the guns. All the guns were smaller than I thought they would be. It had one long pipe where the bullets came out. On the bottom of the pipe was a little sensor and that's probably what is used to aim the guns. Thankfully, they didn't detect anything as small as myself because I wouldn't have been able to make it this close. The main pipe was barely two feet above the ground, and it was being held by another pipe that was mounted onto the ground. Right at the top of the mount was the switch.

"Well, that was easy" I said to myself. I turned it off. As soon as I hit the switch the gun lowered. After I hit the first switch, I made my way to the next one. I was trying to calculate it to see if I would have enough time to turn them all off before I had to make it back, and it wasn't looking favorable for me. There were so many of them and the station was so big. I thought to myself that Tide or Macrill should have come with me, and we could easily turn them all off. Maybe Del didn't need all of them off, so any number of guns that I shut down would be enough for us to get through.

One by one I turned them off, running to the next as soon as I flipped the switch on one. I had done 10 or so already, but my time was coming close for me to turn around. I was almost halfway when I glanced over towards where I came from and saw some-body. I kept running but turned my head in the direction of the person and almost stopped mid-step. It was Truue. He followed me here. I'm sure as soon as he saw us come this way, he knew exactly what we were doing so he followed me here himself. I continued to go from gun to gun shutting off one after another. It was time for me to return, and I had to go back the same way I came other-wise I wouldn't make it. There wasn't enough time to go all the way around, I barely came up short of halfway on the station. As I was running back, I saw Truue hadn't moved. He was just standing above the gun level waiting. I was out of breath and tired, but I knew I had to make it back in time. If I could just run around Truue and not let him slow me down, then I could make it. I made it to the ladder and climbed up. Truue was leaning on a rail to the right of the ladder. He wasn't even in the way of my escape back to the pickup point. I was kinda startled coming off the ladder when I noticed this. He just stood there looking at me. As soon as I got off the ladder I sprinted towards the pickup point. I made it about 10 steps when Truue opened his mouth, "Your mom wanted me to give you this." As I heard him say that my curiosity took over, I turned to look at him. I stopped in my tracks and turned around. I couldn't believe what I was seeing. Truue had our family necklace. It was the same exact one that was always with my mother ever since we fled our home on Zazri. These necklaces couldn't be duplicated. On Zazri molds were used to create these necklaces that almost every Gri family had on Zazri.

"How did you get that?" I said, almost in anger, thinking that he took it from her.

"I'm on your side Skade." Truue went on to say. "I am going to be questioned after you guys' escape." I was caught off guard when he said "escape" as if he knew we would. Truue continued, "Wroff and your mother both knew this would happen. I can't say anything more than that because they'll question me and will be able to tell if I am lying. Ask Tide and Macrill about it when you get back on the ship, they'll explain everything. I know you don't trust me, but you need to take the necklace and Del will pick you up right below here." He pointed down. "I told Del already and we all know you won't make it back in time for the pickup. More ships are coming from Eckles right now and will be here any minute. The guns are going to turn back on any second now as well. Del should be coming up right about now." I was so confused about what was going on and about everything he was telling me. How could he have gotten my family's necklace? How could I trust him after what he just did to us? Truue just seemed so calm and relaxed that it was hard not to at least want to believe him. I went over to him and grabbed the necklace without saying anything and peered over the edge. It was a long way down. Out of the corner of my eye I saw a large group of ships coming towards us. Truue was right. Those must have been the dream catchers coming from Eckles to get us. Then I heard a familiar sound. The Red Racer pulled up just below us, and there was a hatch on the top that slid open. It was only 10 feet down. I looked at Truue who was looking at me. I didn't know what to think or what to say, but we just looked at each other. If Truue really was good, then I think he would understand why I wasn't saying anything. "You've got to go now," he said. I knew he was right as I saw one of the stationed guns start to rise, and I knew that before long they would all be up and firing at us again. With the other ships coming in we would have no chance of escape, so I hopped over the rail and dropped onto the Red Racer. I climbed down through the hatch, and it dropped me right down in front of Macrill and Tide. I looked up just before the hatch was completely closed and saw Truue standing there smiling at me.

Then the hatch closed, and Del quickly took off. We headed straight up through the station and into space. He had to make a few maneuvers to dodge the stationed guns that were now turning back on. I don't know why the other guns were not firing at us while Del was right below us with the Red Racer, but I wasn't complaining. I'd like to think that Truue somehow turned off the other guns. It was a nice thought, but I was still confused about everything that just happened. I headed up to the front and sat down next to Del. "You made it," he said with a big smile on his face. "I knew you would." I looked back down into my hand that was resting on my lap. My family's necklace was in my hands now. I suddenly became less worried about my mother, and felt a little concerned about Truue. He said he was going to be questioned, by who or when I didn't know, but hopefully he would be okay. Hopefully my mother and Wroff would also be okay and the others who were on our side fighting with us in Jacoby and other parts of Ooba.

"Well, off to find your father." Del said to me. I looked up into the space we were entering. It was so different being off Ooba. We had just had the craziest day in our lives on Ooba, and I did not want to go back. Thankfully our ship was fast because I turned around to peer out the back to see all the dream catcher's ships stopped at the station. They were probably thinking that they would have no chance of catching us now. We were in the clear with nothing in our way of reaching my dad. Nothing could be as tough as what we just went through in the past couple hours. I put a smile on my face and for the first time in a long time, I felt hope.

A Little Gri

Space travel wasn't all that unfamiliar to most people. Going from one planet to the next was normal. Most ships were designed to travel through space. Growing up we would often go visit other planets to see friends or to see some new scenery for a week or two. My father typically traveled more than we did, sometimes being gone for months at a time for his work. Whenever he came back, he would always bring us back a little souvenir from the planets he had visited. The stories we heard ranged from funny encounters to terrifying experiences. It seemed like my father always came back a little changed and better because of his work adventures. Occasionally Tide or I would get to accompany him on his shorter work expeditions which were always so memorable and fun. Leaving Zazri and heading to another planet was always thrilling because we didn't know what we would experience next. The things we saw were eye opening in many cases. The things we heard were astounding. The people we met often had great effects on us. And going through the journey traveling through space was always relaxing. We could see so many more planets when we were in space than we could see from being on any given planet. Oftentimes storms on Zazri or cloud cover would prevent us from seeing much. In space though there was just an open area for what seemed like forever. It was all dark, yet it felt so comforting and appealing. The stillness just outside of Ooba and the silence in our ship was a feeling I will never forget.

In the vast distance, we could see other stars and planets. The sight was magnificent. I forgot just how pretty the darkness can be with a little glimmer of light in the distance. I don't remember one time on Ooba when it was dark enough to see the surrounding planets and other stars apart from the two closest stars revolving around Ooba.

There were hundreds of little twinkles all around us. All these planets and stars were always there, but we couldn't see them because of the immediate light from the two stars around Ooba. If I had better vision, I could have seen thousands of other planets, objects, ships, and stars all around. Even being able to see a hundred or so planets in the distance was a sight better than anything I had seen in my days on Ooba.

One thing that I noticed almost immediately was the cool feeling about space. Obviously, it was hard to feel just how cold it was in space being inside a ship, however it looked like it would be a lot, lot cooler than almost anywhere on Ooba. The heat on Ooba was suffocating and it was good to be off that planet. I know better than to assume that I could survive in space and withstand its cold temperatures, but for a second there the thought crossed my mind to go out and let space do its work on me. I wouldn't last too long without the proper equipment, and in all reality, it probably wouldn't be relaxing either, but I fantasized that even for a little bit it would be. Being cooled after years of being on a planet that only knows heat would feel incredible. It was a short-lived thought.

In the distance I saw some reflections of light that were moving a little faster than normal. "What's that?" I said in a startled manner while pointing in the direction of the reflections of light.

"I can't say for certain, but I hope it's not what I'm thinking." Del proceeded to respond.

"What do you mean?" I asked. Before he could respond Tide and Macrill both came to have a look for themselves.

"Yeah, that definitely looks like them." Tide said.

"What do you mean?" I said, "Who's them? And Tide, how do you know about whatever those are?" I knew Del wasn't on Ooba for as long as I was, so he had a better idea of the outside world as it had changed since our time on Ooba, but Tide had been on Ooba for just as long as myself. They both took a deep breath and had a look of great concern on their faces. "Guys, will someone tell me what those are?"

Del finally opened his mouth, "Space Shifters."

He said it as if I was supposed to know what space shifters were. I had no idea what that meant, and I had never heard the term before. "What is a Space Shifter?"

"They are basically a group of people who ransack anything and anyone that they come across for all of their belongings and then they kill them." Macrill said.

Well, that wasn't good news for us. I didn't think there would be other people trying to ruin other people's lives outside of the Clud, but I guess I was wrong. After everything that our universe has been going through since the rising of the Clud, why would anybody else have any desire to inflict more fear and pain into the lives of others, I wondered. I didn't know anything about these space shifters except for what was told to me, and I already didn't like them. During the worst time in our entire universe a group of people want to make it worse for others. Thinking about how Del and Tide knew about them I decided to ask them.

"How do you know about the Space Shifters?" I asked, looking directly at Tide.

"I've just heard about them," Was her simple response. She didn't hesitate to say that, but it did seem like there was more to it that she wasn't telling me. I chose not to pry for any more information, figuring if she wanted me to know she would have told me. "So," I continued, "How do you know about the Space Shifters?" As I looked over at Del. He was still flying our ship in the general direction of Shaker. He looked over at me and just sat there without opening his mouth. I feel like it wouldn't be that hard to tell us how he knew about them, but I guess I was wrong. The pause only made me want to know even more.

Initially I was expecting something super simple like, "Yeah, I just heard stories about them." Or "One of my close family friends encountered them and told me about the experience." Maybe even, "They tried attacking some other ships in our company as we came to Ooba." It looked like he was about to answer when he turned forward again, and his face looked distressed. "They've spotted us," Del said. Whether I liked it or not, it appeared I was going to have to wait to hear his answer. "Strap in, pray they are feeling friendly today." Del said.

We were now much closer to the ships than I had expected. The Red Racer was living up to its name. We were cruising at a fast rate moving along at a great pace. We had anticipated traveling through space for about 8-10 days before we arrived on Shaker, but we didn't account for any extra inconveniences that we were about to encounter. There were only 3 ships that were just cruising through space like us from what it looked like. I wondered what they were doing exactly or what they were looking for, but our ship must have come across their radar as they were now headed in our direction. Their ships had a bunch of reflectors all over them and that's probably why they stood out from so far away. I don't know why they would want to stand out from everything else as that would defeat their ability to surprise attack anybody. The more I thought about these space shifters they didn't seem to be the brightest people.

We were now within firing distance of the three ships. We stopped in our course a couple hundred yards away from them. There we were in open space on a tiny little ship with three people that were super close to me. With our enhanced vision through our ships windows, I saw a random assortment of different races in the other ships. I saw some ugly looking Jubi, which was typical as most Jubi were ugly. Some Lexlands were in their company as were some rubber men with their triangular eye set. It looked like there were some other smaller looking figures in the ship, but it was still hard to point out what race they were. Three ships against one. I like our odds considering we had just escaped about 20 ships back on Ooba. Del looked a little more nervous this time. Nobody was doing anything. We were stopped as were the three space shifter ships. "Deluther!" Came across our intercom in a slow but firm moderately toned voice. Our outbound communications were still down so hopefully they wouldn't be offended by our lack of response. I looked at Del who seemed like he was expecting his name to be called out. I don't know how they knew him or how they could see him so clearly from such a far distance.

Del suddenly pulled on the wheel to slant our ship down and to the left while coming forward just a little then he brought us back to normal. "Why'd you do that?" I asked him.

"It lets them know that our communication system is down." he replied.

"How do you know that?" I asked him, still confused about the space shifters knowing his name.

"Umm, I have just heard about people, who have heard from others and so on about it."

I didn't buy that for a second. There was something he wasn't telling me, and I didn't know why. Why could he not just tell me the truth about him knowing about the space shifters. Before I could ask him again, something came through on our intercom again, "Deluther, we're coming aboard." The voice still sent a chill down my spine. I couldn't see this guy talking to us because they were still too far away, but I just pictured him being very, very, mean looking.

Thankfully, it was up to us to decide who comes on our ship and who doesn't. We just won't let them and that'll be that. Why does he just assume that he can come on our ship without being invited? Also, why would they want to come on our ship anyway? Is this how they attempt to infiltrate every ship they come by? Do they not just shoot us down and then leave? Well, I guess none of these mattered because there's no way we were letting them on our ship. If they wanted to shoot at us, with Del at the wheel we could escape. "Soooo," I said with a long pause, "We going to fly away from these Space Shifters?"

"They're coming aboard," Del said in a very firm voice. He looked right at me and there was no appearance of sarcasm or dispute that would be possible to convince him otherwise.

"What do you mean? Last time I checked, these people only want to destroy everything that they come across and we're just supposed to let them in our ship?" I was so confused. Tide and Macrill both seemed to agree with me. "What?" they both said in amazement from the back of the ship.

"Trust me, they're coming aboard."

Trust me, that phrase only makes me want to question him even more. Is he working with the Space Shifters? Did he lead us here on purpose? Is that how he knows so much about them? Is there a price on our head outside of Ooba as well? I thought Del was good. Was he betraying us? I did not like this, and I knew Macrill and Tide would both be with me on this. I trusted Del up until this point, but now I'm really questioning his motives. Does he have another personal agenda that he's trying to accomplish?

"I'll explain everything if we get out." Del said as if he could read the concerns and questions right from my mind. He said 'we'. Does that mean he's still with us?

"Okay, I trust you," I said to him.

"We all need to move below the entry point of where they will be coming in. They're going to try asking us questions to get out some information and then they may leave, or they may not. Sometimes they are hard to please so just don't say or do anything dumb. Be ready for my signal if things get out of hand and we'll have to fight them off. Be strong, they are very experienced, so we need to work together. I'm guessing only two of them will come aboard and the others will man the other ships. The leader will come aboard and if it comes down to it, we can use him as leverage." Del just gave us a little rundown of what he thought would most likely happen. I felt some assurance that he knew, but it was only assuring because I'm trusting in him. Otherwise, I wouldn't feel comfortable at all with what was about to happen.

The ship was quieter than I had anticipated. They were so far away and then the next thing I knew they were right above our entry hole. Their ship hovered right above ours when a hole under their ship opened. A larger figure was the first one to come down. I couldn't get a good look at who else was coming because the first guy was huge. I didn't think he would fit through our hole honestly, but sure enough he made it through. He dropped down right in front of me. He was a massive Jubi. His hands looked like they'd seen better days, but that's just how most Jubi looked. He had a very muscular, thick-skinned body. He looked right at me but stepped to the side and looked back at the entry hole. Down came a smaller Gri. He must have had some bodily defects because he was smaller than most. He wasn't a kid, but his stature looked like the size of one. It is rare, but sometimes people don't grow the way they should. He dropped down and was just shorter than my waist. He was smaller than I had anticipated. There was something about him that was striking though when he turned and faced me. There was this look in his face that was just evil. At that point I realized that he was the boss and I'm not sure I wanted to know what he was capable of.

"Deluther," the smaller man said, and it was the same deep voice we heard over the intercom, "Come here." Deluther didn't say anything, but walked over and they embraced each other though it seemed like the embrace wasn't genuine or real. I didn't know what Del's path consisted of in the past exactly, but whatever it was, it must have been pretty serious.

"So," the little man proceeded to say, "What are you doing out here with these Gri?"

Without a moment's hesitation Del opened his mouth, "We're just looking for a better life." There was another pause. Obviously, they knew each other, but I wondered if their conversations were always this slow and awkward.

"Well, I guess it doesn't matter what you guys are doing, you know we have to bring you guys in."

"I mean, it wouldn't be the first-time you guys' disobeyed protocols, right?" Del asked, trying to get us out.

The little man gave a little laugh that even sounded dark. "You're right Deluther, however you know we can't just turn a blind eye in this circumstance." He looked right at me which was scary. "Grab him." The bigger Jubi understood immediately and grabbed my shoulder with his arm. The pressure was intense, and I had the feeling that he wasn't even trying to hold on with everything he had. My right shoulder almost immediately started to go numb.

"Hey what's going on?" Tide and Macrill both shouted out. Even a blind man could see the tension in our little ship. Macrill and Tide both started to come at the larger man.

"Hey, stop right there," said the little man, as he turned his back towards Deluther and faced Macrill and Tide directly. "If you want to see him alive you will let him, go."

Then Deluther jumped in and grabbed the little man from the backside. "Let him go," Del demanded from the bigger man. My shoulder felt like it was about to just fall off at this point. "Let him go, and I will let him go." Del started to tighten up on the little guy with his hand around his face and his other arm wrapping around his body. For a second, I felt sorry for him, but then I remembered his look and knew better. I'm sure if the little man could talk, he probably would have said something like "Crush them all," or "Just kill them," or something of that nature.

My shoulder suddenly felt relieved. He loosened the grip, but still had me enough for me not to try and get away. We were facing Del and the little man while Macrill and Tide were both on a different side of us. The room on our ship was pretty small especially when we added these two extra people. Del looked directly at the Jubi holding my shoulder. "Let's make it easy and exchange one for one?" He asked with his voice suddenly calmer than moments before. The Jubi did loosen the grip a little, but he also didn't respond. I tried kinking my neck to look back at him to see what the holdup was, but I couldn't get a good look at him from my tough angle. I wondered why he wasn't letting me go right away, it seemed obvious that that was the right thing to do. I looked back at Del who was looking at Macrill and then Tide. He looked like he was trying to communicate some message to both of them without actually saying anything.

I looked at Tide who was looking at Macrill. They both nodded as if they knew something I didn't. Before I knew it, they both immediately came at the larger Jubi holding my shoulder. With both of their forces combined they were able to push the Jubi backwards and luckily his grip on my shoulder wasn't too tight, so I was freed from him. The adrenaline must have really kicked in for both

Macrill and Tide considering how they managed to move a Jubi who looked bigger than all three of us combined. After staggering backwards a couple of feet, he was about to come at us when Tide held out a gun pointed it right at him. That sight stopped him dead in his tracks.

"Here's what's going to happen," Del said from behind us while still squeezing the little man. "You're going to go up to your ship and we're going to detach and go on our way. You and the other two ships are going to let us go. After we create some space between us, we will let him go. He will be able to survive just long enough for you guys to come get him. If you come after us, we will kill him. You know if he were to die that wouldn't look good for you guys." The bigger Jubi seemed reluctant once again. If the little man would have told him to attack, he probably would have, but thankfully Del still had his mouth covered. The little man didn't look like a man that was to be negotiated with.

The bigger man seemed to finally agree. He went up the exit hole and his ship's entry hole opened for him. "Where's the boss?" was heard from inside their ship before the hole closed. "Here take him." Del said while handing over the guy to Macrill and I.

"We know about your plan," the man said as Del took his hand off his mouth. "You know it won't work, not after this little stunt."

"Cover his mouth, he talks too much." Del told us. Macrill ripped off a part of a cloth covering some supplies and shoved it in his mouth. Del went back up to the front and slowly started to fly away.

"They're not coming after us." Tide said as she was peering through the windows looking at the other 3 ships. Del started to go a little faster. Our plan was working. The bigger Jubi must have told them that we would kill him if they came after us.

It only took about 8 minutes for us to travel far enough away from the other three ships to finally slow down to drop the little man off. We could barely see the other ships now. They hadn't moved at all since letting us go. They were being true to our agreement so we would be true to ours. "You'll have 7 minutes before they pick you up. You'll pass out before then due to lack of oxygen, but you'll be revived without any issues." Del then proceeded to put a little device in his pocket. "You know what this is, if you guys follow us in the slightest, I will set it off." Del took him from us, and I opened up the exit hole. Del pushed him out of it without any resistance from the little man. As soon as he was out Del went back to the front and sped off.

Once again, I felt sorry for the little guy knowing that soon he would pass out due to lack of oxygen and he was probably going to experience extreme cold temperatures. "This was the only way." Del said as if he was reading my thoughts. "He'll survive and we'll probably see him again before we return to Ooba." I had a feeling he was right. We would see that little man again in the near future. Hopefully he remembers us keeping our part of the bargain and allowing him to live.

"What was that device that you put on him?" I then asked.

"It's called a pulser." Tide yelled up at us from the back.

"A pulser? What is that?"

"When the device is activated, it is connected with the pulse that is closest to it, the pulse of the individual becomes the life-line essentially of the pulser. If the pulse of the person is taken away from the pulser it will blow. It can also be controlled by the person who activates the pulser. I have the other part of it and if I push the button then it will blow, and it also tells me the distance between the other part of the pulser." Del proceeded to tell me.

"Why wouldn't they just deactivate or throw the pulser away right away."

"The pulser has a short life and will only work for two days and then it will deactivate and become defective. However, it only needs to be 3 feet away from the pulse for a total of 4 seconds for it to go off. The explosion is very big despite its small size." That makes sense now.

"Why didn't the man struggle or resist being put into space when we dropped him off?"

"The more he struggled, the sooner he would pass out and the harder it would be to bring him back. He needed to stay calm to increase his chances of being revived."

I was shocked after hearing about all of this. Del really was an extremely wise and experienced individual. I didn't know how he knew about all this stuff and how he knew the Space Shifters so well, but I'm glad he was with us because we would not have made it without him. "Wroff knew about your past experiences, didn't he? That's why you were most likely to come on this voyage. More so than anybody else, huh?" I asked Del, now realizing why Wroff trusted him so much.

"Wroff knew, yes. He dreamed about this as well, knowing that the voyage would have failed unless I came." Once again, I was taken back.

"Okay, last question," I proceeded to say, "How do you know so much about the Space Shifters, and why did they know your name?" There was silence. It seems as if Del didn't want to respond. He just stared out the window without acknowledging me or the question. I really wanted to know, but at the same time I wanted to respect his background and history. I didn't know about the sensitivity of talking about his past experiences, but I guess I knew now. After being ignored for a couple minutes I decided not to let it bother me by not knowing. If he wanted to tell me about his past, then he could tell me on his own terms.

"Well, let's go find my father and save Ooba." I said trying to lighten the mood and change the subject.

"Yeah," Macrill shouted from the back. I was glad Macrill was with us, he understood me well and always helped support me when I was in tough situations.

Del looked over at me after the statement, "Yeah, let's go find your father."

About The Author

I was born and raised in the state of Utah. My upbringing was a blend of playing sports and exploring the great outdoors, which instilled in me a profound appreciation for both physical activity and the wonders of nature.

My educational journey led me to Utah Valley University, where I earned my bachelor's degree. During my time there, I developed a deep-seated desire to make a positive impact on the lives of others, particularly in the field of education and personal development. Currently, I'm pursuing a master's degree, working towards my dream of becoming a school counselor, with the aim of guiding and supporting young minds on their journeys to success.

The idea for this book has been brewing in my mind for a couple of years. Drawing from my life experiences and a desire to inspire and empower others, I decided to embark on this literary journey. One day, I sat down with determination and started writing, giving life to the vision I'd nurtured for so long.

www.ingramcontent.com/pod-product-compliance
Lightning Source LLC
Chambersburg PA
CBHW070759160726
48004CB00001B/251